More praise for *Cantora*

"Remembers a history traced back not through men but through women ... Like any good writer [López-Medina] knows stories exist not entirely in the what is said, but in the what is not said—the what is alluded to, or avoided, for the sake of *quedando bien*. And here, between history and conjecture, is where *Cantora* takes flight."

—Sandra Cisneros

"These protagonists are strong-willed women who, despite social constraints, persevere in the pursuit of their goals and personal desires. It is indeed refreshing to see Latina women portrayed as such."

—Erlinda Gonzales-Berry
Author of *Poso Por Aquí*

"Impressive ... The oral narratives of these women create a rare style in contemporary novels. ... *Cantora* should not be underestimated as a novel about traditional Mexican-American culture, the kind we have read before. It can be seen as literature for the turn of the century, a time when present-day writers like López-Medina who know the long history of struggle by their people—especially women—prepare us for the future."

—*Albuquerque Journal*

"Beautifully written ... A poignant story of love, perseverance and survival ... a story of women coming to grips with changes, sometimes accepting, sometimes rejecting, sometimes reverting."

—*San Antonio Express-News*

"At center stage is a unique feminine sensitivity ... one full of passion and knowledge."

—*The Bloomsbury Review*

CANTORA

A Novel

Sylvia López-Medina

ONE WORLD

Ballantine Books • New York

Sale of this book without a front cover may be unauthorized. If this book is coverless, it may have been reported to the publisher as "unsold or destroyed" and neither the author nor the publisher may have received payment for it.

A One World Book
Published by Ballantine Books

Copyright © 1992 by Sylvia López-Medina

All rights reserved under International and Pan-American Copyright Conventions. Published in the United States by Ballantine Books, a division of Random House, Inc., New York, and distributed in Canada by Random House of Canada Limited, Toronto.

This edition published by arrangement with University of New Mexico Press.

Library of Congress Catalog Card Number: 92-97307

ISBN: 0-345-38166-1

Cover design by Georgia Morrissey
Cover illustration by Cathleen Toelke

Manufactured in the United States of America
First Ballantine Books Edition: November 1993
10 9 8 7 6 5 4 3

For my beloved daughter

Adrienne Thérèse

too gentle for this world

and,
for the Concertmaster

reunited in the stars
at the Still Point, my love,
we shall be the Dancers

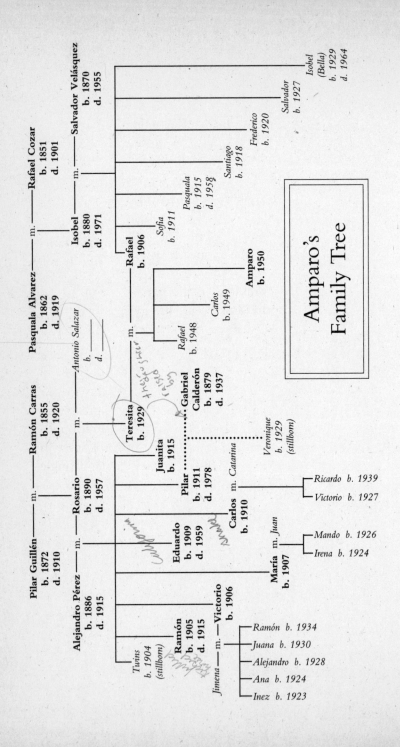

NOTE FROM
THE AUTHOR

The inspiration for this story came from my experiences growing up in California, listening to my family's history, but this is not the story of my life. It is a work of fiction based on the oral history of my family told through the voices of four generations of women. Some of the characters are fictional, but the theme of survival is grounded in reality.

In an age when our technology threatens to race ahead of our human evolution, the dreamsongs of oral tradition can provide the remaining links to our heritage. These links must be treasured and preserved, chained together from generation to generation to create a human bridge of voices. Amparo's story is only one link in this bridge, a mestiza voice; a single facet in a cultural kaleidoscope of memories.

My father was born in Spain, in the seaport of Cádiz. The history of his ancestors travels back through countless generations in Spain. My mother was born in Sonora, Mexico, and the history of her forebears begins as far back as the Mayan pyramids.

I am mestiza. This means more than my declaration that I am one-half Mexican and one-half Spanish, for I was born and raised in California. Being mestiza in the United States means that I have grown up in three cultures, not two.

To grow up mestiza in California, for me, was to grow up living on the edge of irony. It meant growing up in a vise caught between the pride and aloofness of my Hispanic grandmother, and the humility and love of my Mexican grandmother.

For many of us, to grow up in the sixties also meant we cruised, we drank too much at parties, we married young, and then we fell asleep. We slept through the drug scene; we slept through Viet Nam. We became the perfect wives and mothers. The restlessness did not begin until the early seventies when we were kissed to consciousness by the Women's Movement. When we left our marriages, we left to save our lives. We left behind traditions that did not recognize divorce, or a woman's independence. Very little in our culture supported what we did.

But many of us have since let ourselves see that being mestiza means we can be proud of our difference and uniqueness; it means we can be proud of our heritages, for they have enriched us and made us who we are.

Being mestiza means that by being set apart, we have become the observers, thus, we are not lost in the tangled forest of U.S. culture; we are not lost at all.

Sylvia López-Medina
Santa Cruz, California
July 27, 1991

ACKNOWLEDGMENTS

This story could not have been written without the support and encouragement of many of my friends. I would like to acknowledge with love and gratitude the memory of Robert Mognis, Chairman of the English Department at Modesto Junior College. Dr. Mognis handed me my first writing award in the Spring of 1985, thus setting me on my path.

I am indebted to the staff of the English Department at MJC: Paul Neumann, Kathy Shaw, Gary Phillips, Robert Elam, Lee Nicholson and Genevieve Bouwman. I feel a special gratitude to Dan Onorato, both for his dedication to the Celebration of Humanities Arts Competition, and for his unfailing belief in my ability as a writer.

I am indebted to Page Stegner, director of the Creative Writing Program at the University of California, Santa Cruz, for making it possible for me to write this novel; to Porter College for awarding me an Undergraduate Fellowship in order for me to complete my work; to James Houston for his guidance and support, and to his wife, Jeanne Wakatsuki Houston for her kind friendship and encouragement; and to Louis Owens, professor of literature and creative writing, for his perceptive guidance and support during the final stages of this novel, but most of all for being my friend, and for helping me believe in myself. I once heard a lecturer say that the new writers can easily recognize the very best writers, because they want to help us.

To my friends who continued to love me even after I disappeared while writing this novel: Cameo Moore and her beautiful daughter, Hannah Bethany; Marie Clary for being there always; Greg Mellen, Jay McCarty, Steve Smith, and Mitzi Merek, who hang around to see what I will become when I grow up; and Charlette Peralta for her assistance in the final editing of this novel—my love and gratitude. To my sister, Cynthia Fuller, for believing in me and never failing me—my devotion.

To my sons, Paul and Nicholas, who once believed everyone's mother went to college and was a writer; who learned to make their own lunches; and, who are growing up with a sure knowledge of the true value of women in our society. I know I am succeeding when Paul chooses all girls for his soccer team. "They are better kickers, Mom." And Nikki, who is all boy, and who will knock down anyone who tries to change the spelling of his name, and who believes girls can be anything they want. You are both my guiding lights.

I wish to express my gratitude and admiration for Gerald Vizenor, professor of literature, writer extraordinaire, and my renegade mentor, for his belief in me as a writer, his support and encouragement, his guidance, and his friendship more precious than diamonds. Last, but certainly not least, to my editor, Andrea Otañez, without whose dedication and perceptions this novel would never have come to fruition. There is nothing more rewarding than the making of a new friend.

PROLOGUE

1978—Santa Barbara, California

My Aunt Pilar is sixty-seven. Recently, she became disoriented while we were in Southern California visiting relatives. We had driven over the border to Tijuana to shop in the duty-free department stores. While looking at some jewelry, I was temporarily distracted and my aunt wandered out through the door onto the busy street. I was able to quickly get help from the authorities, but their search for her did not end until late that evening when she was found huddled in a doorway seven blocks away.

I visit my aunt more now because of her illness, but when I look at her and sit quietly with her—she no longer recognizes me and we do not speak—I see not a sixty-seven-year-old woman in rapidly failing health, but rather I notice how she is still concerned with her appearance. She does her hair and her make-up. She is meticulous while suffering from an illness that should make her indifferent to her appearance. The doctors tell me this. They tell me what they know, that victims of Alzheimer's return to their childhood in so many ways, that she cannot take care of herself anymore, that we must care for her now. There is so little I can do, except visit with her, and wonder what she is thinking while she sits almost in a trance. I try to share her mind, travel back to her childhood with her, take her home again. I can only do this through my own memories, and hers, related to me over the years and presented now in a secret silence.

There was always a hush when Pilar related the family's history. As a child, I sat quietly while she told me of her memories of the tiny Mexican village where she was born. There are Yaqui Indians in her memories, swooping down into the village, taking food and every young girl they could find. There are villages burned and families moving on to other places to rebuild their lives. There is the love story, the magical love story of my aunt; and there are the brutal deaths of her father and older brother. There is the exodus to western Mexico, a trek by my twenty-three-year-old Grandmother Rosario and her six remaining small children through a mountain range. There is the survival. This is the story of that survival, my Grandmother Rosario's and my Aunt Pilar's.

My name is Amparo. Join me here with my aunt. Sit here beside us. Cover yourself with this quilt. My Grandmother Rosario made it. Warm yourself with it. The mystery of our lives is to be found in its varicolored threads. I will share the tears and the triumphs of these lives. I will show you how to survive anything. We will show you how to survive everything.

PART 1

CHAPTER 1

1904—Chihuahua, Mexico

Rosario Carras waits impatiently, pacing along the river beside the mesquite trees. She cannot imagine what is making Alejandro so late. They always meet here by the river and he is never late.

The sun floating above her is suspended by the stifling heat billowing invisible clouds along the river. Her thick, black hair clings to her neck and back. Lifting her hair with her hands, she tries to hold the heavy tresses on top of her head, but her arms soon weary. Where is Alejandro?

Releasing her hair, she walks the few feet to the river and kneels, placing her hand in the cool current. Leaning forward, she lowers her face into the water. Cold and wet, the water feels like her linen sheets at home, smooth and silky. Rosario turns her face to the side and lifts it, allowing the rest of her hair to fall into the water. The current pulls the entire length of it under the surface. Her hair entangles and catches in the pebbles and vegetation of the riverbed, but her body begins to cool. Crawling into the stream, driven by the searing heat, she pulls off her cotton dress and briefly wonders if the embroidered designs sewn there by her mother will bleed onto the white cotton— cooling her body is all she really cares about. She turns over onto her back and lies full-length on the smooth pebbles shimmering along the bottom of the stream. In her pleasure, she is oblivious to her surroundings, and to Alejandro Pérez standing by the tree watching her. The sun is behind him, causing a shadow to drift onto the pebbles beneath, as if an invisible artist spilled his black pigment into the crystalline water changing it to a blue-gray penumbra over Rosario's drifting hair.

Alejandro shifts his body and his shadow moves over Rosario. Blocking the sunlight, he startles her. She opens her eyes and abruptly sits up, reaching for her dress that is drifting in the stream behind her. When she sees it is Alejandro, she releases her dress. Shameless, she stands and begins walking toward him, the opalescent drops of water falling off her body with each step.

Toward late afternoon, Alejandro let a very tired Rosario slide off the back of his horse. The sun was going down and they were later than usual. She reached up and kissed him and tried to pull him off the horse. Giggling, she almost succeeded.

"Thursday, in the cactus grove? I'll see you then, my heart."

"If I am not there by midday, go home. Do not wait for me."

"Why would you not be there, Alejandro?"

"Tonight I must carry a message."

"For Villa?"

"Yes."

Alejandro sat proudly upon his horse. He had been

carrying messages into the mountains for several months, part of a relay system that traveled across the Sierra Madres to Pancho Villa's stronghold. Villa had been in hiding for eight years since he had killed a man while defending his sister. Now, Villa was not only a bandit leader, but also an advocate of social reform, and his relay system was his only link with Francisco Madero, a champion of Mexican liberalism and critic of Porfirio Díaz.

"You will be careful, Alejandro?"

"The rurales cannot catch us. I should return in two days."

Rosario watched as Alejandro rode west toward the foothills. Soon, he and his horse became an infinitesimal dot on the horizon.

Entering the house through the kitchen in back, Rosario hoped to avoid her mother. She knew her father would be in his study. He was always there this time of day. Her dress was ruined, its colors running down the front and back, on the short sleeves and along the hem. She wanted to reach her room before Juana saw her. She took off her sandals and walked silently on the cool, red tiles, down the hall to her wing of the hacienda. In an effort to avoid the rest of the servants who might be in her section of the house, she detoured through her sitting room.

When she was younger, it was her playroom filled with toys and dolls. Now, since she had turned fourteen, it had been redecorated by her mother to reflect Rosario's transition into young womanhood. The toys were replaced with her embroidery, which she hated. Books substituted for dolls. She didn't understand why. Her tutor, with her since she was five, had been dismissed on her thirteenth birthday.

Carefully, she opened her adjoining bedroom door and looked for Juana. She was hanging towels in Rosario's bathroom, but Rosario didn't see her. Relieved, she walked into her room and began taking off her spoiled dress.

"Little one, where have you been? You are late! Your father is asking for you!"

Rosario turned toward Juana, who was coming out of the bathroom and descending on her like a judgment.

"Look at you! You are covered with dirt! Your hair is a mess! What is this in it? Weeds?"

"I've been playing by the river. I fell in, Juana. I ruined my dress. Please do not be mad at me."

"You must take a bath and wash your hair. Your father is waiting for you. You cannot appear before him looking like this."

"Will you help me with my hair? It is so much trouble. Why can't I cut it, Juana?"

"You know your father would never allow it. Let's hurry. He has been asking for you too long now."

CHAPTER 2

Her hair still damp and braided with ribbons, Rosario, wearing a clean white dress, hurried to the other side of the hacienda and her father's study. As she approached the big double-oak doors, she slowed her pace, stopping with her hands on the iron handles. She took a deep breath to compose herself, as her mother had taught her, and then quietly entered her father's study.

"Good day, Papá," Rosario said formally.

Ramón Carras stood behind his desk looking out of the window. Rosario waited. She didn't move or fidget. Her mother had taught her well. Finally, her father turned to her and held out his right hand. Rosario moved forward and around the desk and bent to take her father's hand. She kissed the back of it as he held it out to her.

"Good evening, Rosario. Where have you been? You are late, my daughter."

"Yes, Papá. I was playing by the river. I forgot the time. Can you forgive me, Papá?"

"Today, I would forgive you anything, Rosario."

Curious, she asked, "What is so special about today, Papá?"

"Today we must talk about your future."

"What do you mean, my future?"

"The future I have chosen for you. The future I chose for you the day you were born. For me and your mamá, it was the happiest day on this hacienda. Did you know, there was a fiesta that lasted three days? We all celebrated, the family, the servants, even the caballeros."

Almost in a whisper, Rosario answered, "No, Papá. I did not know."

"On that day," he continued, "I decided your future. It is a very good future, one that will ensure you are cared for and loved all of your days. Your sons will be heirs to both my estate and to the estate of your new family, the Alcanzars."

"Who are the Alcanzars, Papá?"

"Antonio Alcanzar is my childhood friend. He lived on the adjoining estate next to my father's in Spain. We played together, rode our ponies together, went to school together."

"In Spain, Papá?"

"Yes, Antonio and his family are still in Barcelona. He has a son, Frederico. He is seventeen, now. A fine young man. Antonio writes that Frederico excels in school and will attend the university next year. Frederico is to be your husband, Rosario."

She did not move. Instead, she stood in front of her father and watched him turn away from the window to sit in his chair. He was next to her now, his eyes on her. She stared out of the window, reaching for a peace she felt she would never know again. The sky was beginning to lose its blinding brilliance. Today, the light had spilled over her and Alejandro in the foothills. Everything they had touched seemed to have been bathed in this light. Now, it was fading slowly as her father watched her.

Fighting to maintain her control, she said, "Papá, what are you saying to me?"

"I am saying that it is time for you to leave your mother and me. It is time for you to join your new family in Barcelona. You will live with them until you are sixteen, and then you and Frederico will marry. You will be treated with the same love and caring you have received from your mother and me. You will be very precious to them, Rosario. Frederico is also their only child. They never had a daughter, so they look forward to your arrival."

"My arrival? What arrival? Papá, what are you saying?"

Panicking now, she turned to him. Where was her mother? Why wasn't she here? She won't allow this, Rosario was certain.

"In three days, you will begin your journey to your new home. Juana will accompany you. She will stay with you in Barcelona. She will always serve you and your children."

"Children? What children? Papá, I don't want to get married. Certainly, I don't want to marry a man I do not know!"

"Rosario, this has been decided. There is no one here who would be worthy of marrying you. This is a good and proper arrangement I have made for you, with a family who will love you and understand your needs. There will be no discussion about it. It is decided."

"But, Papá, please listen to me! I do not wish to go to Barcelona! I do not wish to leave you and Mamá! I do not want to marry anyone! Please don't send me away!"

She knelt before him and began moving toward him, her white dress catching beneath her knees. She felt the handmade lace rip away from the hem, but still she kept moving. She stopped in front of his knees and embraced them.

"Papá, look at me?"

Frustrated, he looked out of the window. The sun had nearly completed its descent. In the dusk, the lianas appeared to hover against the cooling adobe walls of the hacienda, as if hiding their faces in shame at what was taking place just inside the window. Rosario was crying, her face buried against her father's legs.

"Rosario, you must not do this. You must be happy. Most of all, you must trust me. Someday, you will realize that what I have decided for you is for the best. You will be grateful to me."

"No! I will not be grateful to you for sending me away! Please, I beg of you, Papá! Please!"

She waited, her face against his leg, her tears drying. He did not reply. Rosario began to feel as cold as the water that rushed over her face that morning. The memory of Alejandro's shadow over her body began to chill her. Always, she had been indulged and allowed to go her own way, to make her own choices. The land that her father owned was so vast; she knew she was safe anywhere she went. The caballeros kept a protective eye on her. Her father's hacienda was her world, and now he was sending her away from it, away from Alejandro. Could he know about their liaison? Had he found out about their involvement with Villa's guerrilleros?

"Papá, how long have you known? Why are you telling me now?"

"I have known since you were born. Frederico was four years old when Antonio suggested this alliance. I realized it was right for you, so we signed the contract when you were three months old."

"A contract, Papá? You signed a contract? Like a business deal? I am one of your business deals?" Abruptly, she pulled away from him.

"No. Not business. Your life, Rosario. It is important to your mamá and me that you be happy and cared for as we have always cared for you."

"Mamá knows about this? She agrees?"

Unbelieving, Rosario stood up and backed away from her father.

"Your mamá knows. Of course she agrees."

Rosario began edging away from her father. She reached behind her and felt the large oak desk. Working herself around it, she found her way to the carpet that covered the center of the room. Against her back she felt the table that held a reading lamp. With her hands behind her, never taking her eyes off of her father, she worked her way around the chair, then she ran to the double-oak doors. Stopping there, she turned and looked at her father.

Her voice low and full of disdain for him, she said, "I don't believe you. Mamá would not send me away."

As she left the room, her father, tense with anger, turned back to the window and stared out into the night.

CHAPTER 3

Running through the hacienda, Rosario wondered where the servants were. Usually, she could never walk through the vast house without encountering one or two of them. Tears were beginning to stream down her face. Wiping them with the hem of her torn dress, she hurried.

She entered the kitchen expecting to find her mother supervising Lupe, their cook, but Lupe directed Rosario to her mother's wing of the house. She tried not to think of Alejandro because she knew she would become confused if she allowed panic to overwhelm her, if she succumbed to the fear that waited like a vicious animal ready to pounce. Her only hope was her mother. Rosario didn't believe she could send her away. What would she do without her in this cold, empty hacienda?

Wiping her face again, she realized her hands were shaking. She stopped and looked at them. Her arms and her body were trembling. She began to breathe deeply, trying to stop her sobbing. Slowly, she regained control. The house was quiet, as if in mourning. She heard only the tick of the clocks that her father kept throughout the house. All of them were imported from Europe and they were his pride.

The heat of the day had vanished now that the sun had descended, and her skin felt chilled and clammy.

Her hair was still damp. She reached behind her head and began to unbraid it. It had been pulling at her temples, giving her a headache. Someday she would cut it. As it fell in cool ripples below her waist, she began to feel the tension leave her body.

She would talk to her mother. Her mother would not allow this to happen. Rosario began to feel confident and headed toward her mother's room, the white ribbons from her hair floating through her fingers to the red tile floor.

As she entered, she did not see her mother immediately, but she knew where to find her. Continuing through the vast room, past her mother's silk-canopied bed, where, as a child, Rosario had jumped, she approached the door to the right of the bed. She entered and joined her mother on the prie-dieu, crossed herself, and accompanied Pilar through the rest of her prayer. When they were finished, her mother kissed the crucifix of her rosary.

"Mamá, I must talk to you! Are you finished with your prayers? I do not think I can wait!"

Pilar turned as Rosario looked into her mother's eyes. As always, she was awed by their beauty. Her own eyes were replicas of her mother's, vast pools of aquamarine. Several generations before them, one of her mother's ancestors formed an alliance with a French soldier and all that was left in evidence of this were their blue eyes. Their faces bore the high, exquisitely carved cheekbones of their Mayan ancestors; full lips and a slightly broad nose completed their heart-shaped visages. Their hair was the rich blue-black of their Indian ancestry. Little of her father's countenance revealed itself in Rosario's, except, perhaps, his stubbornness and willfulness.

Pilar had anticipated Rosario's visit and could see that her daughter was troubled. She had been kneeling on her prie-dieu since Juana had told her Rosario was in Ramón's study.

"Let's go to my sitting room, Rosario."

"Yes, Mamá."

Pilar displayed a serenity her daughter ever hoped to mimic. Rosario had tried many times, but always she failed. It was something inborn, she concluded. Something to which only her mother knew the secret. She needed it now to still her trembling hands.

"Mamá, Papá tells me I must go away. To Spain. Can this be true?"

"Your father and I have always known this."

"But, how can it be? How can you send me away, too?"

Pilar looked down at her hands, for once not busy with her embroidery. She looked back at her daughter, and Rosario could see the resignation in her mother's face. The young girl began to feel chilled again, but she was careful not to display any emotion. So much depended on her ability to convince her mother that this must not happen.

"I do not want to send you away."

Rosario began to relax.

"But, your father has made this decision for us, and we must not disobey him."

Reaching for her mother's hand, Rosario began speaking quietly.

"Mamá, I do not want to leave you and Papá. I do not want to go to Spain. I will not be happy there."

Pilar pulled her hand away from her daughter. She continued to stare at the silken fabric of her dress as her other hand began clenching and wrinkling the material.

She replied in a whisper, "There is nothing I can do, Rosario. This is your father's wish."

Rosario looked at her mother in disbelief. Pilar had begun a gentle rocking back and forth on the couch. Being so young, Rosario did not recognize abject grief, but she did see in that moment her mother's total helplessness. Was she equally helpless? Could she do nothing to determine her own destiny, to change the path her father had set for her? Watching her mother withdraw, Rosario realized she was the only one who could direct her own future. In those seconds, she changed. Without being fully aware of what was happening to her, she reclaimed her dependence on her mother.

Acting on instinct, she said, "Mamá, I understand now. I will do as Papá wishes. You must not worry. I know that Papá and you love me and want what is best for me. I will go to Spain."

Pilar looked at her daughter and saw an earnest innocence. She believed her and immediately stopped wrinkling her dress. Tears of relief began coursing down her cheeks as she took Rosario into her arms.

"I will miss you so much, my little one, but I know this is best for you." Then, in a whisper, she added, "We must not make your papá angry."

"I will miss you, too, Mamá. I will think of you always. I love you, Mamá."

Gently, Rosario disengaged herself from her mother's arms. She stood up and looked around. Rosario had spent so many days in the warmth of this rose-colored room. As a child she had played on the carpet-covered red tiles while her mother had made and embroidered Rosario's doll dresses. In this room she had felt the warmth of her mother's love as a direct contrast to the coldness and aloofness of her father. He gave orders and the entire household obeyed, even her mother. Rosario realized now that it was more than a room to her mother, it was Pilar's refuge.

"Mamá," Rosario said quietly, "I will go now and find Juana and ask her to help me pack my things. We have much work to do. I will come to you in the morning. We will have chocolate together. Good night, Mamá."

Reaching down, she kissed her mother on the cheek. Pilar held her a moment longer, then let go and remained seated on the couch. Pausing at the door, Rosario turned and walked back to her mother.

"Mamá, your blessing . . . please?"

Pilar looked lovingly at her daughter as she knelt before her. She placed her hand on Rosario's head.

"The Lord be with you as you go from me and as you return to me."

Rosario looked up into her mother's eyes and whispered, "Thank you, Mamá."

After Rosario had left the room, Pilar remained motionless for a few seconds, then placed her crystal rosary on the table beside the couch. She held her hand over it for a moment, then abruptly pulled it away, as if she had been burned.

She rose and entered her chapel. Behind the altar, directly below the tortured Christ on the cross, she pushed a lever. A part of the wooden paneling to the right of the altar began to move, leaving a narrow opening in the wall. Pilar passed through it into a small windowless room. She lit a slender white taper on the turquoise-painted altar before her. Using the taper, she lit the thirteen pale blue candles surrounding the statue of the Virgin of Guadalupe. As their flames took hold, the light radiated onto the pale blue walls and a hand-embroidered white linen cloth draped on the altar. Pilar had been closely supervised by her own mother when she, as a child, sewed the ancient symbols in delicate, precise blue and gold threads. Though her family was Christianized by the Spanish priests over four hundred years ago, they had not let go of their ancient beliefs, handing the teachings and rituals down from mother to daughter. When she was little, Rosario had joined her mother and Juana in this hidden sanctuary, unbeknownst to Ramón and his stern Catholic beliefs.

Pilar raised her eyes in supplication to the sorrowful face of the Virgin, then prostrated herself before the altar and began to cry. As her sobbing slowly ceased, she began to chant.

CHAPTER 4

Rosario stood outside her mother's bedroom door and listened to the sounds of the hacienda. She could hear Lupe preparing dinner. Dinner! How could she possibly sit through a dinner with Mamá and Papá? She knew she could not bear it. She must find Juana. No! She would talk to Lupe herself. She hurried to the kitchen.

"Lupe."

"Yes, my little sky?"

Lupe turned to Rosario, her hand stirring the soup kettle in front of her. She was a small woman, barely taller than the pot. She had to reach up, bending her elbow high into the air above the stove.

"Could you send a tray to my room?" Rosario asked.

"To your room? You are not going to eat with your mamá and papá? They will not like this. Are you sick?"

"Yes. No. I mean, yes, I am all right. No, I am not sick. Oh, Lupe, you are confusing me. I have work to do in my room. I must pack. I must decide what I will take with me to Spain. To Barcelona. I am to go to Barcelona in three days."

Lupe stared at Rosario, stunned. Without realizing, she let go of the spoon. It disappeared into the thick, red soup.

"To Spain? You are to go to Spain? Why? What is the matter with you? Are you making fun of me again? Always, you tease, but not this time. You go too far this time. Go now, wash your hands for dinner. Have Juana braid your hair. You cannot come to the table with your hair like that. Indian! That is what you look like! A wild thing! Wild! Your poor mamá. Always worrying about you running all over the estancia. When will you begin to act like the lady your mamá is?"

Rosario backed up against the large trestle table that stood in the center of the room. As a child she had tormented Lupe by stealing pastries from the kitchen and running outside with them to share with the servants' children. She had been a daily nuisance as Lupe moved between the stove and the table. Now, Lupe was advancing on her, scolding her as she had always done.

"Lupe, no. You do not understand. I am to be married in Spain. When I am sixteen. I will go to Barcelona to live with my new family. I must get ready. I must get ready tonight."

Lupe stopped moving toward Rosario, and instead began wringing her hands in her apron.

"Married? Are you certain? Your mamá is sending you to Spain? Your papá?" She whispered in disbelief. "You are not lying to me? This is the truth?"

Nodding her head, Rosario answered, "It is the truth, Lupe." The cook took Rosario into her arms and began crying.

"I will never see you again. They cannot do this to me. What will I do? Who will I cook for? I cannot cook for your children? Your little ones? Where is your papá? I will talk to him. He cannot do this to us."

Pulling herself out of Lupe's clutches, Rosario sought to calm her.

"It is all right, Lupe, Papá does this so that I will be happy. Mamá agrees."

"You are happy you are going? You want to leave me? And Juana?"

"No. I do not want to leave, but I must do as Papá says. Juana is coming with me."

Lupe began crying again.

"Both of you are to go? You will both be leaving me? Ay, Dios mío. How can this be?"

"Lupe, listen to me. I do not want to go, but I must. I will be sad to leave you." Rosario began to cry, too. "I do not really want to eat dinner with my mamá and papá tonight. I just want to be by myself for a while to think about this. Will you please help me? Will you send a tray and tell Mamá that I am beginning my packing, so I can be alone tonight?"

The cook ceased her sobbing and put her arms around Rosario again. Speaking quietly in an attempt to soothe Rosario, she said, "Of course, little one. I will bring your dinner to you. I will not let anyone disturb you, not even Juana. Of course, you want to be alone. Pobrecita, pobrecita."

CHAPTER 5

Determination building, Rosario slowly walked the rest of the way to her room. When she arrived, the room was in shadows as a diffused glow drifted through Belgian lace curtains, creating an island of light on a large wooden chest beneath the window. Beside the chest was a highly polished table upon which stood a small, elaborately framed picture of a young girl in a white communion dress, her lace mantilla framing an angelic, innocent face.

A chair, polished and partially covered with a richly embroidered pale blue shawl, stood next to the table. The fringe of the shawl lay along the shimmering oak floor and trailed to an Aubusson rug where it blended into the pale blue roses and faded green leaves. The carpet continued across the room to a high oak, four-poster bed, canopied with pale blue silk and trimmed with ecru lace.

The rose-pink bedspread, piled carelessly with silk-fringed pillows in shades of lime green, pink, blue, and violet, showed an indentation of Rosario's body, her book half hidden beneath a pillow. The book was open, so that its gilded pages shimmered and reflected off the silk bedspread.

Opposite the bed was a large armoire, and next to the armoire, a massive dresser. On the dresser, an embroidered batiste runner was covered haphazardly with jewelry, including a string of pearls and a gold pocket watch etched with pinkish-gold flowers. The open cover revealed an ivory face and gilded roman numerals. Also on the dresser was a silver-backed, intricately designed hairbrush, a silver comb in its bristles. More pictures in sepia tones were framed in gold.

Unmindful of the shawl, Rosario promptly sat in the chair and waited patiently. An older woman entered carrying a tray. She placed it on the table in front of Rosario and left the room. Rosario methodically ate all the food on the tray, then put it aside.

She walked to her closet and studied the clothes. So few of her dresses would do. She took out a white three-tiered, embroidered cotton dress. She remembered the fiesta early this summer when she had danced in it for her father's friends. She took it off its hanger and laid it on the bed. There were two plain huipiles that Juana had made for her. Rosario always wore them when she helped Lupe with the baking. She took these and placed them on the white dress. She went to the other closet where she kept her riding clothes. In it were three pairs of boots. She placed them and the leather chaps her father had made for her by the bed, then she removed the rest of her riding clothes and put them by the dresses.

She brought a large leather bag from her dressing room and attempted to stuff the clothing and boots into it, but they wouldn't fit. From a dresser drawer, she took a quilted bag and emptied it onto her bed. Doll clothes tumbled onto the silk bedspread, all handmade and hand-embroidered by her mother. She ignored them. Into the bag she stuffed the three cotton dresses, leaving the riding clothes and boots in the leather case.

She went back into her dressing room and put on a pair of riding breeches and a white silk blouse, discarding the white dress Juana had put on her earlier. She then sat on the carpet next to the dress, her blouse still unbuttoned.

What time is it? Where would Alejandro be now? In the hills with the guerrilleros? Maybe. She had no way of knowing. She didn't even know where he lived. Where would she go?

She stared at the rug, tracing the cream-colored roses with her fingers. It's not important where Alejandro is right now. She realized she must leave the hacienda anyway, tonight, right now.

Slowly, she stood up. She surveyed her dressing room. On the oak vanity lay a silver mirror with a raised design of roses on its back. She knew it was very old. Her mother had given it to her on her twelfth birthday; it had belonged to the grandmother who was Rosario's namesake. She picked it up and walked into her bedroom and put it in the quilted bag.

Standing by the bed, she looked around the room until her eyes found the chest under the window. Rosario went to it and lifted the lid. Inside were her shawls. Some were in silk, some were embroidered by her mother. She picked up a black one sewn with tiny pink roses. Then, she lifted out a large cream-colored wool one with fringe eight inches long. It would be warm in the winter. There was a white lace shawl, so delicate it felt like a spider web in her hand.

Her mother had called it Cluny. It was from France. Rosario considered it, then dropped it back into the chest. She closed the lid, returned to her bed and placed the shawls into the cotton bag.

She put on a pair of boots, tucking in the bottoms of her riding pants, then took a leather belt out of a drawer and put it on. Finally, she retrieved her riding hat from a gold hook on the side of the oak closet.

Carrying the two bags, she stood just inside her door and listened. It was quiet in the hall. Her parents were eating. Juana was helping to serve, as she always did. Rosario carefully opened the door and stood outside and waited. She had forgotten something, but she couldn't recall what it was. She waited and tried to remember, then put the bags on the floor and went back into her room.

Walking to the chest under the window, she lifted the lid. The muted light fell on the lace shawl. She held it in her hands for a moment, then wadded it into a ball and stuffed it inside her riding jacket.

She turned and left the darkened, heavily shadowed room. Moonlight, cold and forbidding, entered through the window and fell onto the open chest.

CHAPTER 6

Rosario didn't saddle her horse before leading him out of the stall. Using a piece of leather she found hanging on a hook, she tied her bags together and threw them over the gelding's neck, and then attached a bag of oats and a pigskin of water. She led the horse behind the trees growing alongside the corral. She knew her parents were eating in the dining room on the other side of the hacienda, still she didn't want to risk being seen by any of the servants. She followed the line of trees to the back entrance of the ranch and paused before a section of open ground that led to a gully running the full length of her father's property. Seeing no one, she began walking the gelding across the grass. She reached the gully, climbed onto the horse and began an easy gallop. Soon she was riding the horse at full speed, the bags knocking against his sides.

It took her an hour of hard riding to reach the low foothills. The gelding was in a lather and Rosario knew she would have to abandon him. She climbed down and lifted her bags from the horse, and leaving them tied together, placed them on her right shoulder. She fed the horse the oats and began walking away from him, but he followed her. She stopped and turned around.

"Go home!"

The gelding stared at her.

"Go home! Now! Go!"

He took two steps toward her.

Rosario walked around to the back of the horse. He turned with her. Exasperated, she spoke to him in a normal voice.

"Go back to your stall."

She shoved against the horse with her shoulder. The horse backed away. She hit him on the nose. He backed farther away.

She hissed at him.

"Now, go!"

He looked at her dolefully, then turned and walked away a short distance. Rosario snapped at him.

"Stay there!"

She began moving away from the horse. He stayed where he was, stretching out his head toward Rosario as she took a few more steps away from him. Rosario began walking faster, but the horse remained. She began running, looking at the ground in front of her for the smooth boulders she and Alejandro had walked on that afternoon. There was little light, but finally she could discern the smoothness from the hard-packed dirt. She stayed on the rocks as she progressed further into the foothills.

The gelding remained behind, watching the girl dancing over the rocks, carrying the heavy bags on her shoulders. When she stumbled, the horse whinnied and bared his teeth. Then he turned and began slowly walking back to his stall and more oats.

Rosario soon lost track of time. She was unaware of the cold in her search for the cave she had found earlier with Alejandro. She couldn't remember if it was before or after the large pine tree that stood alone, a sentinel, watching the barren terrain below. She rested against the tree's rough bark for several moments, then decided to search to the left of it. In the dark, she did not know if she could locate the entrance hidden behind protective boulders. Rosario had only found it today because she was certain Alejandro was hiding from her in the big rocks. In fact, she had nearly missed it, but when she was certain it was a cave, she had called to Alejandro excitedly. They spent the rest of the afternoon exploring, Rosario overwhelmed by the adventure of it. She wanted to locate the cave again because she knew Juana would find her gone at first light when she came to wake her, she knew her father would call out the caballeros to search for her. She must not be found.

It was another hour before she discovered the entrance. Tired and dirty, the bags becoming an unbearable burden, she stooped and walked into the cave, dropping the bags on the ground. She sat on a large stone and, in her exhaustion, began crying. She was frightened. Twice she heard rattles, though they were sluggish from the cold. She wondered what else was breathing in the dark. Lizards? Scorpions? She was almost too tired to care. She missed her mother already. And she was cold. Placing the cotton bag against the rock behind her, she lay down and put her head on it. She fell asleep before the tears had dried on her face.

I was seven years old when my Grandmother Rosario died in 1957. When she became ill, I'm certain she must have called one of her daughters living nearby her in Santa Barbara, either my mother or one of my two aunts. When they saw she was sick, they took her to my Aunt Pilar's house to care for her. I remember the color red, but I don't know why. Red is a color I associate with my grandmother's death. Was the house red? Was it the red coat I wore when I was young? Where does the red come from?

I can remember one day sitting on the couch in Pilar's living room. I heard Rosario crying from pain and discomfort, my mother and my aunts in the kitchen discussing what to do. They spoke in Spanish, so I don't know exactly what they said, but I recognized the tones of distress and extreme anxiety. They didn't know what to do; as small as I was, I realized this. I sat on the couch frightened by the alien world of illness, and listened to the whisperings and my grandmother's moans. My father came that afternoon and took me home. Three days later, when I returned from school, my mother was crying. She told me that my grandmother had died. She waited for my reaction. I am certain now in retrospect she was waiting to comfort me. I was afraid and very bewildered, so I remained silent, not knowing what to do.

I wondered what would be appropriate, so I asked my mother, "Is it all right if I cry?"

"*Yes, it is all right for you to cry.*"

I left the couch and like a sleepwalker went into my bedroom. I was crying as I fell down onto my bed. Later, I went to sleep.

Remembering this now, I feel as if I am trying to recall a dream, searching through the mists for whatever it was that was red. Was it the house, my coat, or my grief?

CHAPTER 7

The next morning when Juana discovered Rosario's disappearance, she ran through the house crying out her name, searching for her. When she told Rosario's father, he immediately sent a message to the village asking for help. A two-day search revealed that her horse's hoofprints ended at the edge of a vast outcrop of rock. Many hundreds of yards of this rocky terrain lay at the foot of the low rising mountains that Alejandro and Rosario had explored two days earlier. When Alejandro returned from his journey, he joined the search. He suspected she had returned to the cave, but he was afraid to ride in that direction, lest he alert the searchers of her whereabouts. He knew she had run away, and that her father was determined to find her, but no one knew why she had fled.

They searched the first day and through the night, and then through the second day without any luck. On the second night the fatigued searchers gathered in the yard of the patrón to await his instructions.

He came out of the house and stood on the upper steps of the large tiled porch. Torchlight flooded the yard, so Alejandro moved back into the shadows. He had avoided the patrón during the search, not knowing if he had found out about them, not knowing if this was the reason she had disappeared. "Caballeros, good friends. My wife and I both wish to thank you for your help in the search for our daughter. I know you are all tired and hungry. Tonight we will not search. We will wait until first light tomorrow morning. My daughter must be found. Her mother has become ill with her grief. She cannot be comforted. Until tomorrow morning, good night, and my gratitude to each of you."

Ramón Carras stood on the porch and watched the men slowly leave the yard. He nodded to one of his neighbors, waved to a group of his caballeros, then turned and slowly walked into the house, proud, stern, and forceful. When he had closed the door behind him, he walked across the darkened entry to a settee against the wall to the right of the door. He slumped onto it and held his head between his hands.

His wife was bedridden; Juana and Lupe hovered about her night and day. The house was silent, empty. He no longer had any idea where Rosario might be. He did not know where to begin the search in the morning. In the recesses of his mind he kept avoiding the one possibility that could destroy him: Was Rosario alive? Was she injured somewhere, alone in the night, afraid?

He got up slowly and stared into the darkened entryway, then walked down the hall to his study. He entered, crossed the room, and sat in his chair. Staring at the floor in front of him, he remembered Rosario kneeling there two days before, her arms wrapped around his knees, begging him not to send her away.

Looking closely at the floor beneath his boot, he noticed a piece of white lace. He reached down and picked it up, holding it to the light of his desk lamp.

When he recognized it as a piece of lace torn from his daughter's dress, sobs from the bottom of his soul began erupting, rising through his chest, beyond his control. One followed another, overlapping until he felt he would choke on them. In an effort to keep anyone in the house from hearing him, he pressed the lace against his mouth and placed his head on the desk. He remained there for most of the night, his muffled sobs tearing through the silence and echoing their way to Pilar's room.

Juana and Lupe, sitting by their mistress's bed and watching over her fitful sleep, heard the sobs and stared at one another in helpless fear.

CHAPTER 8

The darkness forced Alejandro to dismount. He remembered clearly the group of flat boulders that
marked the edge of the rocky terrain. With little
moonlight to provide shadows, Alejandro knelt and
scanned the gently rising hill before him. He could
not see the boulders. Finally, he decided to move toward the left and scan again. There appeared to be a
tree in that direction, and from his kneeling position
he could barely make out its naked spire against the
dark sky. Wasn't there a tree just like that outside the
opening to the cave?

He had said good-bye to no one, not even his
mother or his younger brother. He was certain that
Rosario's father did not suspect him, but if he eventually did, Alejandro wanted to make sure his mother
could not give them away. Soon, he would get word
to her. For now, he knew he must find Rosario. Did
she have any food or water with her? Just in case, he
had taken as much from his mother's kitchen as he
could carry. He had no money, but his main concern
was to find Rosario. The only place left to look for
her was the cave.

The flat boulders rose gently before him. They
looked soft to the touch. He had no light, but he
carefully felt his way around the rocks and finally
found the opening to the cave.

"Rosario," he whispered. "Rosario, are you in there? It's me, Alejandro. Rosario?"

There was no answer.

The cave was so dark, he couldn't see anything. Again, he knelt and began to crawl in carefully, feeling his way inch by inch. He had gone about ten feet when he felt Rosario's riding boot. Awakened and startled, she cried out.

"Let go. Let go of me!"

"No, Rosario, don't be frightened. It's me, Alejandro."

"Alejandro! Oh, you are here! I can't see you!"

Reaching out his hands in the darkness, he gripped her shoulders, and continued until he had his arms around her. Rosario placed her arms about his neck.

"You're here, I am not dreaming." She touched his face. "I have had such strange dreams in this cave, Alejandro. I dreamed that I had died here and that you found me."

"Rosario, I have been so worried and scared. Your father has been searching for two days."

She stiffened.

"Does he still search? Last night, I saw the torches. I was so frightened. They came near several times, but no one found the cave. Are they still searching, Alejandro?"

"No, not tonight, but they will begin the search again tomorrow at sunrise. Have you eaten, did you bring food?"

"I brought only water. I could not bring food. I still have water, but I don't feel too well."

"Here, I brought food from my mother's house."

She ate hungrily as Alejandro continued. "Why did you run away? What happened? Your father is very distressed and your mother is ill with worry."

Between bites she told him about the plans for her future. Alejandro did not move or interrupt her. He grew appalled and angry as she spoke.

"You were right to run away, but why didn't you tell me? Does your father know about us? Does he know about the guerrilleros, or the messages we carry?"

"No! He said nothing about the guerrilleros. He talked only about my marriage. I was so frightened, afraid I would be caught. I had to trick everyone." She paused. "Even my mother. I lied to my mother."

She fell against him, but had no more tears to shed.

"It is all right, Rosario. It will be all right. I am going to take care of you now. You mustn't be afraid anymore. We will go from here to a village I know about. It is about three days away. I have friends there. They will hide us."

"But, Alejandro, I sent my horse back to the stables. How can we ride three days on one horse?"

"Yours is here with me. I took him out of your father's stable. Can you ride now? We must not wait too long. We only have about six hours of darkness."

"Alejandro?"

"Yes?"

"Are you scared?"

"No! Are you?"

"Yes, a little."

He hesitated, feeling around the small cave for her bags. She rose to help him. As they fumbled around in the dark, he spoke, barely above a whisper.

"Actually, I am scared. We'd be stupid not to be."

"Alejandro?"

"Yes," he replied, beginning to lose patience with her.

"I'm glad you came for me. I'm glad you found me."

He could barely hear her. He put down her bags and pulled her close. She clung to him and he could feel her trembling.

"You did the right thing to run away. I could not live without you, Rosario. Now, let's go."

I used to visit my Grandmother Rosario when I was a little girl. In her backyard there were three very large eucalyptus trees. They stood guard along the property line and I believed they were my friends. One was very old and pruned so that the trunk was level and squat. I couldn't put my small arms around the tree, resigning myself to hugging the other two, but I would often climb to the top of the stubby tree and sit on the leveled surface, looking out at the neighborhood. When my grandmother discovered me there, she would scold me in Spanish as I climbed down. I had no words in Spanish to explain to her the security I felt nestled in the concave of the old tree.

When I was in kindergarten in 1956, I attended a school in Santa Barbara a few blocks away from her house. I had lunch every day at my grandmother's and, as I approached her street, the scent of the eucalyptus would greet me.

She always made chicken soup with rice. We could not speak to one another, because of our language barrier, but I would sit at the table while at the stove she ladled out a bowl of the soup. In my memories, I stare into the golden broth, the steam warming my face. She stands and watches me eat my lunch, smiling at me, solicitous. When I finished, we would clear the table, then she would pat my head, straighten my dress, and lead me into one of the bedrooms where she had created a private altar. This one was different from the one she kept in the living room. I liked it better. The white, embroi-

dered altar cloth was very old. It was torn slightly in places, more the result of age and wear than of any kind of abuse; the fabric was yellowed in spots so that the pale blue candles, when lit, cast ivory reflections upon it.

Standing behind me, Rosario placed her hand on my head in silence while I looked in awe at the face of a virgin I did not recognize. The face of the virgin in church was painted a pale pink, her face benevolent and filled with love. This visage was brown and sorrowful. My grandmother would bless me in Spanish, chanting the benedictions, filling the room with magic. She would light a match, place it in my small hand, and guide it to an unlit blue candle. As the flame caught and burned, I would turn and look up at its reflection on Rosario's face. As small as I was, I realized this was a holy place for my grandmother, more sacred than the sacristy in the church we went to every Sunday. In moments like these, my Grandmother Rosario instilled in me the reverence the nuns had attempted, but failed, to teach me in catechism.

Often, I visited my grandmother with my parents, but these midday visits my first year of school were the only times I can remember being alone with her.

Now, all I need is the scent of eucalyptus and I remember vividly my grandmother's house, the bedroom and the ivory candlelight, the magic and the mystery. I also know now that in the act of lighting the candles, Rosario was bestowing more than a blessing. Her love burning in the gentle flames bequeathed to me an inner power that would help me secure my own liberation. But I didn't know then that in my adulthood I would always seek her in the flames of blue candles and find my autonomy in the memory of her blessing. Instead, I would return to school every day with this one reality: my grandmother loved me.

PART 2

CHAPTER 1

1915—La Cruz, Mexico

Pilar tried to turn away from the dirt as her mother continued pressing her face into it. She was only four and small for her age.

"Mamá, you are smashing me. I can't breathe!"

"Pilar, be quiet! They are coming into the church. Be quiet!"

Whispering, Pilar replied, "Mamá, you are too heavy on me. Please."

Rosario moved slightly so she was no longer leaning on Pilar, but she made certain she was still shielding her from the eyes of the Yaquis. Rosario had not dressed Pilar like a boy today, nor had she for several days. She had relaxed her vigilance because it had been weeks since the indios had raided.

She looked at her friend, Consuelo, hovering next to her inside the confessional and peeking through the curtain at the approaching Yaqui. He was armed with a large hatchet, and followed by several other Yaquis into the church. A group of women and children huddled behind the priest who stood in front of the altar. He held a crucifix in his hand while he bravely confronted the leader.

"What do you want? This is the house of God and

these are only women and children. There are no
men here. They have gone to the next village."

The Yaqui ignored him. He surveyed the people
clustered about the priest until his eyes fell on a
young girl of twelve. She was dressed in the white
cotton pants and shirt of the village boys and her hair
was cut short, but it made little difference. There was
no mistaking the delicacy of her features.

He approached the priest and stared at him for several seconds. Pilar watched from the hiding place in
the confessional as the tension grew in the priest's
face. The women and children moved closer to the
padre, but the Yaqui was indifferent to their fear as he
turned toward the young girl. Fascinated, Angelina
 never took her eyes off him. He reached toward her
as her mother tried to protect her. Taking her by the
arm, he tried to pull her toward him. She resisted.
Her mother began to scream and claw at him, but he
pushed her aside and pulled on the girl's arm again.
Angelina resisted once more, and he hit her across the
face. As she began to fall, he caught her and lifted her
into his arms. She struggled, but he turned and carried her out of the church. Her mother screamed until she collapsed on the stone floor of the nave. The
other women rushed to her side.

Pilar could feel her mother trembling. She turned
to look at Consuelo, who was holding Pilar's baby sister, Juanita. Her older sister, María, was huddled,
trembling, in the corner of the confessional. Five-
year-old Carlos was trying with difficulty to see
around his mother, but Rosario continued to hold
him behind Consuelo. The moment the alarm had

warned the villagers that the Yaquis were coming again, Rosario and Consuelo had carried the children, running toward the church. They listened in fear as the Yaquis went systematically through each small house, looking for food and valuables. They always came to the church before they left the village and then took one or two of the young girls. Pilar and her older sister, María, had grown up dressed as boys most of the time, as had every girl in the village.

My Grandmother Rosario gave birth to nine children before she reached her twenty-fourth year. The first two children were twins who died shortly after their birth. She then gave birth to her oldest son, Ramón, named after her father. Very soon there followed my Uncle Victorio, Aunt María, Eduardo, Carlos, Pilar, and Juanita, the baby.

When Ramón was ten years old, he and his sister went to the village store on an errand for his mother. Aunt María remembered him as a very obedient boy. He was Rosario's pride. There was a group of older children gathered on the street looking for entertainment, and when they saw Ramón, they began teasing him. He chose to ignore them and continued into the store with María. When they came out, the older youngsters were still there. They circled Ramón, taunting him.

One of them had a new horse and invited Ramón to ride it. He refused, saying that he had to go home and ask his mother's permission first. They laughed at him and together lifted Ramón and placed him on the horse. One of the boys slapped the horse on the rump and it began running. Ramón had never been on a horse, since the family was too poor to own one. He immediately fell from the saddle, but his foot caught in the stirrup. He hung along the side of the horse as it ran, his head banging on the ground. By the time some of the men in the village had stopped the horse, it was too late for Ramón. He was dead.

María would never talk of what took place after they un-tangled Ramón from the horse and carried him home. We only know that this happened two weeks after Alejandro, their father, had died.

CHAPTER 2

Pilar would never forget the dust billowing about the streets in the wake of the Yaquis leaving the village. It was a few weeks after Angelina had been taken, and Pilar, her mother, and the other children were returning from the hills where they had hidden when the alarm sounded. After the last raid, the priest insisted the villagers no longer hide in the church. Ramón, Victorio, and Eduardo had gone to the next village of San Marcos with their father to trade, as they did every month. As usual, Rosario and the rest of her children had stayed behind.

As the woman and her children approached their street, Pilar noticed a small gathering of villagers in front of her house. She soon realized they were the men who had gone with her father. There was someone on the ground and Ramón, crying, was standing next to the body.

Pilar's mother began to run toward the men. Rosario handed Juanita to María so suddenly that the baby awoke with a jolt and started to wail. María sat down to try and quiet her; Pilar ran after her mother. When the little girl reached the crowd, Rosario was on the ground next to Alejandro. His face was very pale, a blue tinge around his mouth. He was trying to talk to his wife.

"Don't try to speak, Alejandro. Just rest. We are going to carry you into the house."

Rosario was calm, but Pilar, at the age of four, knew her mother always became very calm the more frightened she was.

"Rosario, I thought you were dead. Some of the villagers told me you and the children were dead."

"No, my heart, we are not dead. All of us are well. We were in the hills behind the village."

His breathing became more labored and he appeared to be in great pain. She looked up at the crowd of men standing by Alejandro, silently questioning them. Subdued, they held their hats to their chests. Tomás, Alejandro's closest friend, and the one who had helped them when they had arrived ten years earlier, was crying and trying to tell Rosario what had happened, but he kept breaking down. Rosario turned back to Alejandro. She took him in her arms and began to rock him gently.

"Alejandro, my love. We are all here with you," she whispered. "Ramón, your son, he is here. Pilar, your little light. Look, she is here."

Rosario looked up at Ramón and Pilar and motioned them to come closer. Ramón, sobbing now, knelt on the other side of his father, but Pilar could not move. Her mother's face was covered with tears and Ramón had buried his face in their father's side. The little boy was trying to say something, but Pilar could not understand him. Her father's eyes were closed, but Pilar could see his labored breathing.

Suddenly, Alejandro opened his eyes as if he had

been startled. He searched around until he saw Rosario. His eyes riveted on hers.

"Rosario, the children! What will you do? How will you care for them?"

"*Shhh*. We will take care of them. You and I. You are going to be all right. We are going to move you into the house when you feel stronger. We are just waiting. Are you ready now?"

"Rosario, there is a great pain in my chest. I cannot move my arm and there is a cold feeling in my body. I am dying, Rosario."

"No! You are not going to die! I am here with you. I will not let you die."

Rosario, her body tense, gently lay Alejandro's shoulders and head back on the ground. She looked anxiously at the other villagers as more of them returned from the hiding place and joined the gathering crowd. Pilar began to move away and accidently backed into Consuelo, who had just forced her way through the people to be near Rosario. Consuelo knelt and put her arms about Pilar, but Pilar was unaware of it. She could not take her eyes off her mother.

Rosario was straightening Alejandro's clothing, and talking to him in a low whisper. He whispered back to her, and once they even chuckled together briefly, sharing a secret, as Pilar had seen them do before.

They had always been close, sometimes to the point of shutting out their children. Other times they had been childlike themselves in their teasing. No depth of poverty had taken away their love. But Pilar sensed this was one adversity they would not overcome. Her father was dying and Rosario was trying to prevent it through the power of her will and love.

Tomás had brought a blanket and silently covered Alejandro after he had begun shaking. Ramón had not moved, keeping his face buried against his father's side. Rosario was still whispering to Alejandro, when his body began to shudder. Ramón looked up into his father's face, his eyes flooded with tears as Alejandro silently mouthed something that Pilar could not hear.

The shuddering stopped and Rosario pulled Alejandro to her. She buried her face in his neck and did not move for a long time.

The crowd began praying, and the priest arrived with the other women and children he had just escorted from the hills. He immediately knelt down next to Ramón and began the last rites for Alejandro. When he had finished, he touched Rosario on the shoulder, but she did not respond. Concerned, he watched her for several seconds, then turned to Ramón. He lifted the little boy to his feet and led him away.

The crowd began to disperse and Consuelo handed Pilar to another woman standing next to her. The woman took Pilar across the narrow street to her house, and from there Pilar watched as the villagers turned toward their homes. Consuelo knelt next to Rosario, not touching her, not even looking at her, and took out her rosary and began praying.

Pilar stood in the doorway of the neighbor's house until after dark, watching her mother silently rocking her father's body, Consuelo kneeling next to her, saying her beads.

The day of my Grandmother Rosario's funeral in 1957 was cold and windy, one of those first bright October days of autumn. My mother, Teresita, did not know how to drive a car, and my father, Rafael, had urgent business to attend to early that morning, so my mother, brothers, and I took the bus to the cemetery. We arrived too early. The bus let us off two blocks from the entrance in front of a row of low buildings.

One of the buildings was a restaurant that was closed. A mechanic's garage next to it is still there today, and there was a flat-roofed house next to the garage. The house was painted a very pale pink and it seemed to me that it sat halfway into the ground, as if the builder had wished to burrow into a warm place, out of the cold.

We stood in front of the pink house, the wind an icy blast blowing a brutal path through our grief. I wore a dress, my red coat, and knee-high stockings. The wind stung the backs of my legs.

We heard a woman calling from behind us; she was standing in her doorway beckoning to my mother. Inviting us in out of the cold, she had such a look of kindness and concern that my mother accepted.

Sitting in her living room, which looked and felt like a cozy animal's den, I slowly began to warm up. My legs stopped shivering and I was soon able to bend my fingers. The woman offered my mother coffee, and they talked in

Spanish. I did not understand what they were saying, but I knew from the woman's look of sympathy that my mother was telling her of her own mother's death. I don't remember how long we waited there, but finally it was time for us to walk the two blocks to the cemetery.

The funeral homes had not yet implemented the idea of a closed coffin before a burial, so the family stood around the grave, the fresh dirt bruised with shovel marks, and the coffin open for the funeral farewells. My mother was stoic, but my Aunt Pilar and my Aunt Juanita were crying.

I was frightened. I had not attended the rosary the night before and this was the first time I had seen a dead person. My grandmother was dressed in a very pretty beige dress with blue flowers printed all over it. A light blue shawl was about her shoulders. The white collar of her dress was trimmed in lace, and her hair was softly combed back into the braided bun she had always worn. She was asleep and she appeared to have a look of objection on her face, almost as if she were sulking at God for taking her.

The priest said his prayers in Spanish and then the funeral director prepared to close the coffin. We took turns walking past Rosario, showing our last respects. We were all composed, when suddenly my Uncle Eduardo, who had been devoted to his mother all of his life, tried to climb into her coffin. I was now terrified as I watched the rest of the family pull him away. My Aunt María held him as he sobbed and wailed when the funeral director closed and locked the coffin. Throughout all of this the wind was merciless. Only my grandmother had found comfort.

After the family left the cemetery my father met us at our house, where we all shared lunch and memories of my grandmother. As soon as I was able, I crept away to my bed-

room and curled up on my bed and fell asleep. It had been a bewildering, cold, and exhausting day.

For years I would drive by the sunken house many times and remember the lady, her warm living room, and her kindness. But even today, if I should pass by the cemetery where my grandmother is buried, I am haunted by the tragic scene of my aunts and uncles pulling Uncle Eduardo away from the coffin.

CHAPTER 3

Unprotected and alone, Rosario Pérez took her children home. Her fear of the Yaqui raiding and the constant searches through the mountains by the rurales for Villa's revolucionarios became unbearable. Two weeks after Ramón's death, she packed what food they had and began the journey to her father's hacienda, which lay at the base of the foothills east of Chihuahua. It was an exhausting and frightening trek. Rosario's children would retell the story to their descendants many times. They would describe the village where they were born, the dusty streets, the desolation, their poverty, and their endless fear.

As Rosario led the way, Victorio carried the food and María carried the baby. Pilar held her mother's hand and Eduardo and Carlos followed their older brother. It took them three days to arrive at the low foothills Rosario and Alejandro had crossed ten years earlier. When they finally reached them, she paused, relieved, looking for the cut in the canyon through which Alejandro had led their horses. It took her another half day to find it. By then, she and the children were exhausted. She decided to camp at the base of the canyon that night, and then resume their return home in the early morning.

There were about two hours before nightfall, so the children played tag among the mesquite and cactus. Victorio found a dead rattlesnake and teased the girls with it. Rosario sat before the fire where she was cooking their dinner and watched them.

Her grief held in abeyance for three days, she began to feel a force greater than her will pushing her from behind, daring her to give in, lose her balance, and fall into despair. She knew she could not. She had to get her children home to her father and mother, home to Juana's ministrations, home to warmth and security. Only when she arrived would she surrender herself to her grief, tumble with it into her feather bed, lose herself as Alejandro was lost forever beyond her reach and love.

She listlessly stirred the bubbling pot in front of her and listened to her children laughing and playing. Soon, she could watch them run and play around her father's hacienda. She would take out her beloved dolls and give them to her daughters. Her sons would have ponies to ride, and someday a comforting peace would descend upon her. But now, there were the children and the trek home. She need not trouble herself beyond that.

They slept the stone sleep of exhaustion and awoke early the next morning. Victorio had started a fire and Rosario warmed the leftover dinner. After they had eaten, they began walking the last few miles home.

As they emerged from the canyon, Rosario knew she was on her father's property. She and the children had walked all morning and the sun was becoming unbearable, when she finally made out the shimmering lines of her father's hacienda.

"There, you see, 'Torio. Over there. Your grandfather's house. Soon we will arrive."

"I think I see it, Mamá. It is so large. It looks like a small city."

"It is a small city. Many people live there. Many people work for my father."

"And it has a church. Look, there is the cross standing among the trees."

"No, that is our family cemetery. It has been there for many generations. My grandmother and grandfather are buried there, but two chapels are inside the hacienda, one for the priest to come Sunday mornings, and another smaller one in my mamá's wing of the house. It is very beautiful. It is where my mamá prays. It is where I learned to pray."

Remembering all of this, Rosario hurried her step. By the time they reached the outer gates of the hacienda, she was well ahead of the children. She approached the arched entrance and paused. Leaning on the wall of the arch, she could see that nothing had changed. Some of the caballeros were milling about the yard, and she could hear one of them trying to break a horse in the corral as the rest of the men were either cheering or jeering at him.

Rosario began to feel the peace she had been waiting for as the children gathered around her, suddenly shy in their fatigue.

She took Pilar by the hand and began to cross the vast yard. Juana was sweeping the porch and had just turned to clear the dirt beneath her broom when she caught sight of the woman and children.

Juana had aged. At forty-four her hair was gray and

she had gained the weight of her years, but the spirit and determination Rosario had always respected were still evident in her eyes as she trained them on Rosario. Stunned, she crossed herself, but still she did not move. Rosario, coming nearer, broke into a run, pulling Pilar along beside her. Juana recognized her at just the moment Rosario threw herself into her arms.

Pilar became caught between the two women, momentarily squeezed breathless, the sound of their tearful reunion muffled to her ears. She wanted only to squirm her way out from between them.

When she succeeded, she found herself gazing up at a tall, stern man. He stood just inside the door of the hacienda and, shiny in his black garments, he frightened Pilar. He stood as if he had been in the military all his life, his back straight, rigid. She surveyed him with her large blue eyes as he slowly surveyed her. Pilar did not know she was the image of the grandmother for whom she had been named, but he recognized her.

Ramón Carras was dressed in a white silk shirt with a cropped jacket trimmed in silver. His pants fit his slender figure like a reptile's skin, while his black boots rose to just above his knees. Pilar had never seen boots like this. She froze and could not take her eyes off him. His glance burned into her, imprinting forever on her memory the image she would describe nearly fifty years later to his descendants.

Gazing at the little girl, Ramón felt the agony he believed he had put to rest four years earlier when his wife died. She had died begging him to find Rosario, begging him to forgive their daughter for running away, refusing to believe she had run away with Alejandro. He could not promise to forgive Rosario, and so could not allow her this last peace. It was a peace that would forever be elusive to him, too. Now, the child before him was like a visitation from Rosario's mother, a judgment and a condemnation. Her blue eyes were the same aquamarine as her grandmother's. In the few seconds while he stared at this little Pilar, he remembered the first time he had seen the young woman who became his wife.

He had gone to church one Sunday morning, the first time in the many months since his father's death. During those months, he had seldom left his parents' home in Monterrey. He didn't want to be in church that day, but his mother had prevailed upon him, so he sat in the back, begrudging every word of the Mass, begrudging the priest his presence. Suddenly, there was a movement several rows in front of him. It caught his eye, but little of his attention. Then, the movement repeated itself. He looked and saw a young woman, her white mantilla falling off the back of her head. She reached up to adjust it, but it slipped off the other side. Her duenna frowned at her, but the young woman fell into giggles and finally took off her mantilla. The duenna turned, grabbed the mantilla from her, and sternly placed it upon her head again, but not before Ramón could see the blackness of her hair. The light from the stained-glass window at the end of the pew fell on her hair and turned it into a rainbow of purples and blues. Ramón was intrigued. She fidgeted again and her duenna rose and pulled her out of the pew. As they left the church, the duenna furious, the young woman glanced about, her eyes falling on Ramón. He felt as if he had been slapped.

Her eyes were brilliant, large, and knowing. They were not the eyes of innocence, but rather of impertinence and intelligence. As the duenna pulled her past Ramón's pew, Pilar looked at him with a fun-loving smile full of mischief. It was a smile that marked Ramón's emergence from the grief that had overwhelmed him for months.

He asked his mother to find out who the girl was. Pleased to see her son's curiosity return, she learned what she could and told him that Pilar had been convent-raised and only recently returned home. Was she contracted for marriage?

"No," his mother said, "she is to return to the convent soon to begin her novitiate."

Ramón went to the priest. He told him of his intentions to marry Pilar, and asked for his intervention with her family. It took the priest ten months to convince the family that Pilar should be married and not confined to a convent. During the six months before their wedding, Ramón was only allowed to visit Pilar in the presence of her duenna and her grandmother. It was agony for Ramón. He could not touch her, and she would not look at him, but only answer his questions with a whispered, "Yes, Señor," or "No, Señor."

Ramón had loved and ruled over Pilar for the twenty-one turbulent years that ended in her death at the age of thirty-eight. He had not known how to love her any other way. He had given her everything he could think of to make her happy, but he had not planned on giving her a rebellious daughter who would break her heart. His unforgiveness showed in his eyes as he turned his face toward Rosario and her children.

"Papá, it is me, Rosario. I have come home to you and Mamá. I have brought my children, your grandchildren. Here is Victorio, María, Eduardo, Carlos, Pilar . . ."

"I have no grandchildren. I have no children. You must leave now. You are trespassing."

Ramón Carras turned to go into the house. Rosario, stupefied, ran after her father. She grabbed him just as he proceeded through the door of the hacienda, but he shook her off with a violent twist of his arm. Pilar watched her mother stand behind her grandfather as he continued into the house. With her hand, Rosario stopped the door from closing, and followed her father into the house.

"Papá, Papá, it is me, Rosario! It is me, Papá, your daughter. I have come home. I have brought my children. Please, Papá? Look at me!"

"I told you, I have no children. I have no daughter. My daughter is dead. Go away."

"Papá, where is Mamá? Is she in her room? I must go to her. She will know me."

Ramón pushed Rosario away from him again. He seemed to grow smaller in Pilar's eyes. She was standing on the porch now, drawn toward them, her curiosity overwhelming her. Rosario was screaming at him.

"Papá, where is Mamá? Let me pass! I must see my mamá! She will know me! Let me pass!"

Ramón took Rosario by the arm and forced her back to the front door. Before he pushed her through it, he spoke viciously to her.

"I said, I have no children. I have no grandchildren. My wife is dead! Now, go from here. You are trespassing!"

With these final words, he pushed Rosario out onto the front porch with such force that she fell against Juana. In shock, Rosario allowed Juana to support her; she would have fallen otherwise. Slowly, as the realization of her mother's death coursed through her, she crumpled into Juana's arms. Pilar remained riveted to the porch, watching her grandfather. He looked from Rosario to the children, and then his gaze again fell on Pilar. He saw in her eyes the same intelligence and willfulness he had seen in the eyes of his bride that long time ago. He knew that in that moment he would die soon, and that when his time came, he would fall into the same aquamarine-diffused light he now saw in Pilar's eyes.

In his coming senility, he would insist to the servants that his wife Pilar had come home, that she was standing outside on the front porch, waiting to be welcomed. He would demand over and over that they go to the door and let her in. They would repeat the pantomime almost daily during his last months of life.

Finally, he died alone, believing he was at the door and Pilar was running into his arms.

CHAPTER 4

Juana stood on the porch holding Rosario. It was a few moments before Rosario's sobbing ceased, as she began to realize her children were watching her. Slowly she disengaged herself from Juana's arms and turned to look at them. Pilar was standing beside her, looking up into her face, frightened. The rest of the children were grouped together in front of the porch. Rosario realized they didn't know what to do next. She looked at the closed door of the hacienda. Reaching to take Pilar's hand, she walked, a blind woman, down the steps and through the yard to the entrance. The rest of the children followed her.

Realizing they were leaving, Juana ran into the hacienda. She knew she would find the old patrón in his study.

"She is leaving! Patrón, you must stop her! You cannot let her leave with the children!"

Ramón Carras sat in the chair behind his desk and did not answer Juana.

"Patrón, you must hurry. Bring them back! They are leaving the estancia!"

Still, he did not answer her.

"They will die! You know they will die. They are your grandchildren! The little one. Her name is Pilar. You must go out there now and bring them back. Patrón? Answer me!"

Ramón turned his back on Juana. In frustration, she ran out of the room and rushed down the hall to the front door. She looked out to see Rosario and the children rounding the front corner of the adobe wall that surrounded the hacienda. She knew where Rosario was going. Juana then hurried to her room at the back of the house and gathered her few belongings.

Down the corridor from her room was Pilar's suite. Juana nervously opened the large carved oak door and entered. The drapes had been drawn during the years since Pilar's death. No one, not even the other servants, had entered since that tragic day.

Pilar's rosary was still lying on the table by her bed. Juana picked it up and examined it. Made of Austrian crystal, it sparkled gently in the dim light. Going to Pilar's dresser, Juana opened the top drawer and took out one of Pilar's batiste handkerchiefs. The edges were hand-rolled by French nuns, and the lace was handmade. Juana carefully put the rosary in the handkerchief.

She went to Pilar's dresser, picked up an exquisite tortoise-shell comb that Pilar had always worn in her hair, and added it to the rosary. Pilar's jewelry was still in the top drawer of her dresser. Juana put the handkerchief down and opened the velvet box. The emerald necklace that Pilar never wore Juana placed aside. There were Pilar's pearls, meant to be given to Rosario on her wedding day, and the rose quartz pearls saved for a future grandchild. Juana placed these next to the emerald necklace. Unable to determine what other pieces might be of value, she decided to take all the jewelry with her, and placed the emeralds and the pearls back inside the velvet box and put the box beside the rosary.

She knew she must hurry, so she ran to the prie-dieu, reached above it, and pressed below the crucifix. The panel did not open immediately and Juana had to press repeatedly. The panel sprung forward stubbornly and Juana went inside Pilar's small blue room.

That's odd, Juana thought, Pilar's bedroom had sustained a film of dust over every surface, but this room seemed untouched by time. She stood quietly in the center of the room, then, with reverence, gathered the altar cloth around the candleholders and tied them together. The elaborate icon of the Virgin of Guadalupe, her visage more that of the Indians of central Mexico, Juana removed carefully from the wall. She carried the things back to Pilar's room and placed them on the bed.

Back at the dresser, she reached into the middle drawer and searched through Pilar's shawls. She was looking for the pale blue angora shawl the señora always wore to Mass. Yes, there it was. Startled, she felt something small and cold beneath the shawl. It felt like metal. Juana pulled it out of the drawer. It was a small pistol, the kind of pistol a woman carries in her purse. Where did Pilar get this? Did Ramón get it for her? No, Ramón would not give her a gun. Why did Pilar have it? Reaching back into the drawer for the shawl, Juana felt a small cardboard box. She brought it out with the blue shawl and found that Pilar had bullets for her gun. Even in her rush, Juana puzzled over her discovery. Many nights she had heard Ramón and Pilar in loud discussions after Rosario had run away, his voice booming through the corridors, Pilar's pleading with him. There was little peace between them after their daughter disappeared.

After a moment of contemplation, Juana took the gun and the bullets and, with a shudder, put them back in the drawer. The rest of the things she placed in one of Pilar's leather purses, then she left the room.

Juana had come to the estancia as a young woman to serve the patrón and his new wife. She had been nervous and frightened, not knowing what his wife would be like. Would she be kind? Would she be stern and aloof? Would Juana be happy here? She soon discovered that her fears were for nothing. Her new señora was just as young and frightened as she was. Out of loneliness and need, they had become good friends. Together, knowing so little about babies, they had raised Rosario, fussing over her, spoiling her, and loving her.

When Pilar had died, grief-stricken and inconsolable over the loss of her daughter, Juana plunged into a loneliness she had not known was humanly possible. She had stayed at the estancia, knowing that in time Rosario would return. She longed for this, longed for Rosario's children and the laughter that they would bring to this austere and silent house. Now, they were being driven out by the unforgiveness of the old man. What foolishness! What stupidity!

She hurried to the kitchen and began gathering food. The new cook, whom Juana had never liked, began to object, taking food away from Juana and trying to put it back on the shelves of the pantry. Juana took her by the shoulders and pushed her against the wall.

"Get out of my way, puta! Do not interfere with me!"

In shock, the cook stood against the wall, never taking her eyes off Juana. She watched her place a large sack of dried beans in her bag. Juana then poured all the cornmeal into another flour sack and added it to the beans. She took a container of lard and a slab of bacon from the cold room. The cook had just finished making three dozen tortillas and a large pot of beans for the caballeros' dinner. Juana added the tortillas to her parcels and looked around for a container in which to place the beans. Finding nothing suitable, she placed a clean cotton tablecloth onto the table and put the pot of beans in the center of it. She then gathered the corners of the cloth and tied them around and above the pot. She tested its strength and then swung it up to her shoulder. Gathering the rest of her parcels, she left the kitchen.

Juana rushed out through the back door of the hacienda and ran as fast as her parcels would allow. The bacon kept banging against her leg, but still she hurried. When she got to the stables, she quickly took Pilar's horse out of its stall. She went to the back of the tack room and retrieved the harness for the pack animals. She put it on the mare, then expertly arranged her parcels of food onto the animal. Leading her through the yard, she stopped at the well to fill several pigskins with water. She loaded as many of them as she felt the mare could carry, then led her out of the yard toward the family's cemetery.

Rosario was kneeling outside the fence surrounding her mother's grave, her children gathered about her. Juana stopped several feet away and waited. The cemetery was silent and embraced by a hot, dry wind coming from the North. Juana absorbed the peacefulness of it as she listened to Rosario.

"Mamá, I am here," Rosario whispered. "I've come home. My children are here with me. I've brought them home, too. Here is Victorio and María. And here is Eduardo and Carlos, and Pilar. Mamá, Pilar is named after you. She is so like you. And the baby. Here is my baby, Mamá, Juanita. I named her after Juana. I've brought them home to you."

Rosario continued kneeling in silence, her head bowed. Pilar stood beside her, the dry grass along the black, wrought-iron fence rubbing against her bare legs. They itched, but Pilar did not move to scratch them. The air was hot and dusty, the breeze pushing the grass back and forth against her calves, but still she did not move.

There was a stone marker on her grandmother's grave, but Pilar could not read the engraving. Instead, she studied the small glass dome on the marker. Within it, embedded as if held prisoner, was a picture of her grandmother. She was very pretty and very young. Pilar did not realize that it was a picture of her grandmother taken on her wedding day. She only saw the face of a beautiful young girl who looked so much like her mother.

Juana could see that Rosario was about to collapse. The young woman had begun sobbing again. Juana stepped forward and began to gather the children away from her mother. First she took Victorio by the hand and led him over to the mare. She lifted the reins and handed them to him. Puzzled, he stood holding them. Then, she took María over to Carlos and told her to take his hand.

"I am placing you in charge of Carlos. Take care of him."

She gathered the rest of the children, except Pilar, who was by then holding her mother's hand, and began to lead them out of the cemetery.

Pilar watched them go, and then turned back to look at her mother's face. Rosario let go of Pilar's hand and opened the wrought-iron gate and entered. She knelt at her mother's grave and reached over to kiss the picture.

Before she rose to lead Pilar out of the cemetery, she spoke one last time to her mother.

"Mamá? Your blessing? Please, Mamá, your blessing."

She bowed her head, her hand caressing her mother's gravestone. Then, she stood and led her children away.

The Continental Divide meanders its way like a dawdling child south through New Mexico. It continues as the Sierra Madre, and as an afterthought travels the length of central Mexico, ending finally in a presumed state of exhaustion in Cuernavaca. Rosario was born in the outlying area of Chihuahua on her father's hacienda, located near the foothills of this mountain range. She did not want to return to the village where Alejandro had taken her. He was gone, her oldest son buried beside him, and she could not face living there without them. She also did not know how long the revolution would continue. For years the rurales had invaded the villages in the mountains, seeking Villa and his supporters. She had followed Alejandro from village to village, always hiding with him in fear for themselves and their children. Now, she was unable to cope with the hardships of the revolution, nor could she face the continuing battle with the Yaquis, who raided the villages as regularly as grief.

Many nights before his death Alejandro had shared his dream to take her and the children away from the Yaqui raids to a town west of the mountains. "Hermosillo," he had whispered to her. Now, determined to make Alejandro's dream her reality, she turned away from her father's hacienda and headed west toward the vast mountain range before her.

Decades later, my Aunt Pilar told me the story of this trek through the mountains. I sat on the floor in front of her, listening, large-eyed and fascinated, as she wove about me a tale of terror, exhaustion, and relentless thirst.

"How old were you, Aunt Pilar?"

"I was four years old, maybe five. I don't remember exactly. I was little. I had very short legs."

"Weren't you scared? Were there wild Indians? Lions and tigers?"

"No! There were no lions and tigers. You have too much imagination, Amparo. You are silly sometimes."

"Well, then what was there? Did you have dolls?"

"Of course I did not have dolls! We were very poor. We did not even have enough food to eat and never enough water."

"Why didn't you return to the village where you were born?"

"Mamá didn't want to go back there. She was afraid of the raiding by the Yaquis."

"What are Yaquis?"

"The Yaquis, Amparo, were the indios who lived in the mountains. They would raid the villages. They would take food, and they would take the young girls."

"Why would they take the girls?"

"I don't know. I was only four years old, but I remember them."

"What did they look like? Were they scary? Did they have war paint?"

"No, they did not have war paint. They were not at war with us; they only wanted food and the young girls."

"But, what did they look like?"

Pilar studied her hands and the handkerchief she held while she described the Yaquis, only occasionally glancing her fear at me.

"They were tall."

"Taller than Uncle Victorio?"

"Yes. And they had blond hair."

"No they didn't! Indians don't have blond hair, Aunt

Pilar. In the movies, they have black hair, or brown hair. They don't have blond hair!"

She studied me for several minutes, growing exasperated.

"Amparo, these indios had blond hair. They were tall. I remember that. They did not call themselves Yaquis. They called themselves Mayos."

"That doesn't make sense! If they called themselves Mayos, then why do you call them Yaquis?"

"Because, when the conquistadores arrived, they asked one of the indios who they were. He answered, 'I am here.' In Spanish, that is pronounced 'y'aqui.' So, they called them Yaquis."

By now, I was thoroughly confused.

"But, why did they take the little girls?"

"I don't know. My mother dressed María and me like boys. I seldom wore a dress while we lived in that village."

"You wore pants, boys' pants?" I was shocked. I had not yet discovered the convenience of jeans.

"If we wore pants, it made it more difficult to see that we were girls."

I contemplated this, trying to identify with her fear, but nowhere in my safe world could I find a direct corollary. On many rainy afternoons, I curled up on the carpet with a pillow under my head, Rosario's quilt wrapped around me, as Pilar wove a tale of what was to become to me a story of adventure and daring. In my five-year-old world, I was allowed to go only to the grocery store a few doors down the street, but my Aunt Pilar, in my eyes, was a glamorous figure. She had survived a journey, a journey that she placed in my memory for the rest of my life.

CHAPTER 5

Foothills of the Sierra Victorino Mountains

It rained the first night. The high mountains above them had eaten the sun like an avaricious animal, leaving them shivering and miserable in a cold shadow. Rosario and Juana searched desperately for a stand of trees, but in the foothills there were only bushes and scattered cactus. In the distance, Juana thought she saw some boulders, so she hurried the children toward them. Nestled together as closely as possible, they spent the long night with the rain running down their necks and wetting their underwear more quickly than their outer garments.

They were also hungry, as they had not eaten since early morning. Because of the rain, Juana could not build a fire, so she carefully prepared cold beans and tortillas for each of the children. They ate their soggy meal in despair.

The next morning the rain stopped. They were surrounded with mud, but Juana and Rosario roused the children, fed them some more cold beans, and got them on their way.

During the following days, they had to deal only with the foothills. It was a gentle climb. The children scrambled around the rocks, played hide and seek, laughed and teased one another. They were on an adventure that soon made them forget the rain and misery of the first night.

Rosario and Juana chose to stop early one afternoon when they discovered a small stream that flowed into a natural basin about eight-feet wide. The basin overflowed on one side and ran off into another stream below. It was perfect for the children to bathe, so they eagerly began wading in. Juana gathered what few pieces of wood she could find and piled them beside a large rock. She dug a hole and began filling it with small pieces of kindling. When she had a good fire going, she began to cook cornmeal mush for dinner.

Rosario sat nearby, exhausted and discouraged, watching her children. She nursed the baby while Juana cut up some bacon and tossed it into the bubbling cornmeal.

That night, after the children had fallen into an exhausted but satisfied sleep, Rosario and Juana each took their baths in the basin. It would be the last time they would have an abundance of water during their journey.

They traveled through the lower elevations, circumventing the mountains, weaving their way through canyons, but Juana and Rosario knew their options were becoming fewer. Finally they were forced to begin their trek up into the mountains. Juana carried the baby and led the horse. María took Carlos by the hand. Rosario held Pilar's hand, and Victorio led Eduardo. The children were excited. They looked forward to swimming, more adventure. They were several days away from exhausting their supplies and their water. The fatigue that would plague them would not begin for another day, but the beginning of the most serious hardship was only moments away.

Pilar had let go of Rosario's hand and for the past hour dawdled behind the others. Tired, her little legs raised dust with every step. Choking on the clouds billowing about her, she tasted dust and spit it out. Ahead of Pilar, Carlos had complained to Juana who reprimanded Pilar to stop kicking up the dirt. Wearily, Juana continued up a short rise in the path, and around a large boulder.

As Carlos passed the boulder, a change in his pace alerted Pilar. Through the dust, she watched Carlos slow to a stop. He was staring at something beneath the outcropping of rocks piled just above the boulder. He did not move. Pilar caught up with him and followed his line of vision. There, beneath the rocks, swarming over each other, moving as if formed of one body, was a nest of baby rattlesnakes.

Driven by the curiosity of a five-year-old boy, Carlos made as if to reach for them. Fascinated and speechless with fear, Pilar watched him move his hand closer to the nest. She wanted to tell him to stop, but she could only watch helplessly as Carlos took a step nearer.

They did not see the small rattlesnake, coiled and separate from the nest. He was sunbathing on a boulder to the left of the nest. His markings camouflaged him perfectly. Only the subtle sound of his immature rattles gave any hint of his presence. He watched Carlos move closer to his brothers and sisters. Suddenly he tensed his small body, coiled tightly, aimed, and struck Carlos on the left temple. Stunned, Carlos fell back as Pilar began to scream.

Juana whirled about, and seeing Carlos lying on the ground beneath the boulder, ran back and knelt beside him.

"Rosario! Hurry! Bring the bag from the horse. The small, red leather bag."

Taking a knife from the leather sheath she wore on her belt, Juana briefly inspected the blade. There was no time to worry about its cleanliness.

"Pilar, you must hold your brother's hands. You must hold them like this, tightly. You must not let go! Do you understand me, Pilar?"

Mutely, Pilar nodded and took Carlos's hands. He was already unconscious, and she could feel the tremors working themselves down his arms. She watched as Juana crossed herself.

I was playing one day with the children who lived next door to my Grandmother Rosario. It was about 1955, and I don't remember their names. One was a girl several years older than I. She had a bicycle, and I was riding on the back of it, holding on to the seat. We rode it up and down the sidewalk in front of both houses, then we would ride it up my grandmother's driveway and into the empty garage.

The garage was built of old, weathered, dark brown planks. We could look through the spaces between the planks, peek into the gloom, survey the dirt floor and the sparse weeds that grew there. Sun motes shone down at an angle through the spaces, lending light like a blessing into the scary darkness. At the age of five, I knew that monsters filled that garage at night, frightening even the blessings away, but in the daytime the light protected us.

We rode the bicycle up the drive and into the garage, turning it around, wobbling and nearly losing our precarious balance. It was late afternoon, and I noticed how each time we circled in the garage, the light would lessen. The monsters were awakening.

We circled again, but this time I leaned over too much and we fell. My ankle caught in the spokes before the tire ceased turning, and the spokes cut into the heel of my foot, making a deep gash. The pain radiated all the way to my knee. On the dirt floor now, I began screaming as I realized blood was gushing from my foot, forming a muddy red puddle beneath me. There was no more sunlight coming into the garage; the only light came from the open doors.

I saw my grandmother run in with my Aunt Pilar. Rosario looked at me crouched on the ground, saw the blood and began to run around the walls of the garage. I remember thinking, "Why is she waving her arms? I'm bleeding! Why is she running around in the garage like that?" Aunt Pilar was slowly backing away in horror at what she saw. My grandmother yelled something at her in Spanish, but Aunt Pilar didn't move. She yelled at her again, and Aunt Pilar turned and ran out of the garage. Rosario knelt beside me. In her hand was a wad of what appeared to be cotton. I realized too late what it really was. She had gathered spiderwebs from the walls, and she was pulling my hands away from my injured foot. I tried to crawl away from her, but she wrapped one arm around my shoulders and held me still. I began screaming louder, cringing from her. She never said a word. Instead, her concentration focused on getting my hands away from my foot and placing the wad of spiderwebs into my cut.

When she succeeded, the pain stopped instantly. The bleeding ceased and I began to relax against her. My screams turned to sobs and Rosario, speaking to me soothingly in Spanish, picked me up and carried me into the house. Soon, my mother arrived with Aunt Pilar, and they took me to the doctor. He cleaned the wound and stitched it closed.

Years later, after I was grown, I would tell a doctor about the spiderwebs, and he and I discussed curanderas, Indian herbal remedies, and love, and faith.

CHAPTER 6

Juana cut into Carlos's forehead, across the two small marks made by the baby rattlesnake. Blood spurted out, spraying Pilar, covering her dress, getting into her eyes. Crying now, she held onto his arms, watching helplessly as Rosario ran to them and fell on her knees beside Carlos. She opened the leather bag and poured out the contents on her skirt. Blood from the cut was spilling onto the ground and began to soak into Rosario's dress. She looked at Juana, terror in her eyes, silently pleading to know what had happened.

"A snake. He was bitten by a snake."

Juana was calm as she watched the blood pour from the wound and the color slowly fade from Carlos's face. Finally, she decided it was enough. She took a cloth bag from Rosario's lap and opened it, revealing a profusion of dried, brown herbs. Taking a handful, she poured the herbs into the cut. She added more, and kept adding until she was satisfied the cut would not begin to bleed again. Rosario had begun to tremble. Her entire body was shaking and she had begun a low keening, as if a scream were struggling to escape her body.

"Rosario, be still! Be quiet. You must help me. I need a clean cloth, something to wrap these herbs so they stay in the wound. Go to the horse. Find me a cloth!"

Rosario scrambled up from the ground and ran to her mother's horse. She opened one of the saddlebags only to find a profusion of the children's dirty clothing. She pulled them out and kept searching the bottom of the bag. There she found the Cluny lace shawl she had taken with her as an afterthought the night she had run away. It was clean. She ran with it to Juana and watched as she wrapped it around Carlos's head. The entire left side of his face was turning an ugly purple that starkly contrasted against his deathly pallor. Pilar realized his arms had stopped trembling. Was he dead? She loosened her hold and looked up at Juana.

"Did you see the snake, Pilar?"

"Yes."

"How big was it?"

"It was small, a baby. Very small. It went away."

Pilar began crying.

"He tried to touch the other ones. Is he going to—?"

"What other ones? Where? Show me." Juana stood and waited for Pilar to lead her to the nest.

Rosario bent over Carlos and lifted him into her arms. Calling to María, she instructed her to lay a blanket on the ground, and then she placed Carlos on it.

Pilar pointed and Juana looked with hatred at the small, slithering snakes. She located a large, flat boulder, stood over it, and squared her legs. She bent and lifted the boulder, and staggering with it, carried it over to the nest. With a grunt, she threw it onto the snakes, killing them instantly.

1958—Santa Barbara, California

"Aunt Pilar, Juana sounded mean."

"No, Amparo, she was not mean. She was strong. She had to be strong."

We were sitting at the kitchen table in Aunt Pilar's kitchen. Rosario had died the year before. Her small house was sold and her few belongings and her mother's jewelry were divided among her daughters.

"She sounded mean and scary."

"Scary. Yes, she was scary. I was afraid of her. We all were afraid of her. Even my mother. But, Juana kept us alive. She wouldn't let us die. She wouldn't let Carlos die."

"But, Aunt Pilar, he was bitten in the eye by a snake. Why didn't he die? In the movies, when you are bitten by a snake, you die."

I fell to the floor and writhed and pretended to gag. Then I lay still, dramatically dead, lying there like Snow White, the movie I had seen the previous week.

Pilar looked down at me on the floor, a bored expression on her face.

"Amparo, get off the floor. You are getting your dress dirty."

I sat at the table again, and began playing with the small bowl of fresh, green chile peppers we had picked from her garden that morning.

"He was not bitten in the eye, Amparo, he was bitten on the temple above his eye."

"Well, then, why is he blind?"

"Because, the snake venom must have damaged his eye. That is why the eyelid doesn't blink properly."

"Does it hurt him?"

"You mean, does it hurt him now?"

"Well, yes. Now . . . and then, did it hurt him then?"

"Now it doesn't hurt, but then? Yes, it hurt him very much. He cried from the pain. Even when he was not conscious, when we thought he was going to die, he cried. I remember listening to him cry through the nights. Mamá never left his side. I watched her. As the days passed, she stopped being frightened for him. She became calm, strong. Like Juana. She was not going to let him die, either. When he was burning with fever, Mamá and Juana made him a tea from leaves in the red bag. They had to pour it into his mouth. He could barely swallow. Most of it spilled onto the ground."

"I bet it tasted yucky!"

"Amparo, go outside and play!"

Her patience with me again lost for the moment, I went outside, and, for lack of anything to do, I walked on her chile pepper plants, crunching and popping the bright green peppers, watching them ooze into the dirt beneath my black patent-leather shoes.

Eventually bored with that, I went back to the house and looked through the screen door. My Aunt Pilar was still sitting at the kitchen table, staring at the embroidered cloth, her hands held together as if in prayer.

CHAPTER 7

Juana and Rosario hovered over Carlos for many days. The rest of the children stayed nearby, huddling together at night against the cold, sitting quietly and watching Carlos during the hot afternoons. María did her best to cook, according to what she remembered from helping her mother in the past. Victorio saw to it that they had enough wood, though there was little vegetation about them. He would disappear each morning and return later carrying a few sticks. Every morning he would be gone a little longer.

One morning in his search for wood, he discovered a small village. He approached it carefully from behind the rocks only to find it deserted. He walked through the silent, narrow paths to the center of the clustered dwellings until he found the well he was searching for, but it was dry. He returned to the family's encampment and told Juana and his mother about the village. After that, he and Eduardo posted themselves to keep watch for approaching Yaquis.

Soon, Carlos became delirious. He talked, but he did not make sense. Juana continued to pour the tea into his mouth while Rosario held his head. Twice, Juana cleaned the wound and placed new herbs in it. She tore the shawl into shreds, each time finding a clean place on it to wrap his forehead.

Finally she said to Rosario, "We must move him.

We cannot stay here any longer. We are running out of food and water."

"But, if we move him, he will die."

Juana looked with pity at Rosario. It was the first emotion she had allowed herself since Carlos had been bitten.

Lifting him gently, she stood up.

"We are not going to let him die, Rosario."

Rosario led the horse and Victorio herded the children behind Juana, who led the way toward the crest of the mountain range. It took them several more days to reach it. Juana carried Carlos the entire distance. He was a small boy for his age and he would grow to be a diminutive man. His children would adore him. His oldest son, Victorio, would be killed in an automobile accident and his favorite son, Ricardo, would die in Viet Nam, a highly decorated Green Beret. Carlos would never recover from his second loss. He would die soon after Ricardo's death, his living room filled with pictures of both his sons. For now, though, he was a little boy fighting for his life.

It took the family nearly three weeks to walk out of the mountains. Whenever they came to a small village, Victorio and Juana would enter cautiously and ask for food and water. Uncertain of their welcome, only the two of them ventured into each small enclave of huts, while Rosario hid the rest of the children. The villagers would share what little they had with the travelers, give them advice and direction. Water was scarce, but every village had a well from which they could replenish their supply. Several times the travelers dared to creep close to Yaqui villages, only to find them deserted.

Victorio felt his mother's determination to keep Carlos alive. He understood that if they lingered in one place too long, they would risk his death. He could see that the poison from the snake had taken its toll on his little brother. He had not regained full consciousness since the snake bite, his breathing was often uneven, and many nights Victorio had seen his mother and Juana hover over him as the rest of the children slept. In each village, he and Juana asked if there were someone with more healing knowledge than Juana, but each village was too small. Doggedly, they all followed Rosario. Victorio was so afraid of Juana now, that he didn't dare let the children lag behind. Exhausted himself, he carried Pilar on his back and forced María and Eduardo to keep walking.

He became the head of the family at the age of nine, and would never let go of this rule. Unlike Carlos, Victorio would ride his own children, herd them, drive them, so that in their adulthood, two would become teachers, two government officials, and finally, his youngest, Ramón, would become an attorney.

Finally, in the foothills of Sonora, Rosario's family could see a village, the bell tower of the church glistening white, a beacon beckoning to them. After traveling several days without food, their water gone for two days, they continued plodding toward the bell tower and the village it promised. They reached it at sunset.

As they entered the small pueblo, an elderly man

leading a donkey noticed them. He saw an old woman staggering with the weight of a small boy. The boy's head was bandaged, and the woman was followed by several very dirty children. The tallest boy was carrying a little girl. Her dress was covered with blood. Behind the children was a young, slight woman carrying an infant. They walked past him as if in trance.

He ran after them and, taking the young woman by the shoulders, sat her on the ground. He hurried ahead to the old woman and, gathering her and the children, led her back to Rosario. From his burro he took a pigskin of water and starting with the bandaged child, he began to give them water.

Some other villagers joined him, and together they took the family to the church. The priest, amazed by what he saw, led them inside. In the confusion, Victorio lowered Pilar to the floor. She woke amid glowing candles at the foot of a statue of the Madonna. Had they died? Was she in heaven? She heard her mother crying, and turning away from the statue she saw Rosario holding on to Carlos as a woman tried gently to take him. Rosario became hysterical and tightened her grip. The priest put his arms around her shoulders and began speaking to her softly. She loosened her hold, and the woman lifted Carlos and carried him from the church. Juana followed her.

"Aunt Pilar, did you grow up in that village? Did you have friends to play with? Did you have dolls?"

"No. I did not grow up there. We stayed for many, many days. Weeks, I suppose. I did not have friends. I never had dolls when I was a little girl."

"Not even one doll?" I replied, in disbelief.

"Not even one. We didn't stay there. The village people and the priest brought us back to health, but my mother wanted to travel to another village, one my father had told her about. It was called Hermosillo. So, we went there. It was not too far and the villagers gave us plenty of food and water. It was not a hardship, not like the mountains. Nothing was like the mountains. Carlos was better. He could walk, but he tired easily. He could not see from his left eye, and the eyelid would not blink or close properly, but he was alive. The priest told my mother that it was faith and miracles that saved him."

"I thought it was Juana's medicine that saved him. The medicine in the little red bag. Aunt Pilar, didn't Juana save him?"

"Yes, of course she did. But the herbs were good for the cut. They were good for the fever, but they could not save him from the poison. For that we needed faith. We needed to know that God would save Carlos. Juana believed this. We all did. Herbs were not enough." The curandera needs God too.

CHAPTER 8

1915—Hermosillo

"Rosario, this town does not look like much. Why are we here?"

"Alejandro has friends here."

Juana stopped walking, causing Rosario to pause also. "Why are you stopping?" Rosario said as she turned back toward Juana.

"You brought us here because Alejandro has friends here? This does not make sense. We could have stayed in the village by your father's estancia. We had friends there!"

With a fierce determination, Rosario walked the few steps between her and the older woman. She stood with her face directly in front of Juana's.

"Don't ever mention my father to me again, Juana. Do not mention him to my children. Do not speak his name. Do you understand me?"

Juana, eye level with Rosario, sized up the young woman. Rosario did not move, nor even blink her eyes. The calm blue of her pupils slowly changed to a steely gray.

"You must not hate him, Rosario. He is a foolish, stupid old man. He does not know better. He loves you, he just does not know how to show you."

"Love! He never loved me! He never loved my

mother! He owned us. Owned us! Don't talk to me about love. What I ever learned of love, I learned from Alejandro and my children. That is love, Juana!"

"So. Now. What do you intend to do with these children you love, Rosario? What will you do to feed them?"

"I will find something. I will do something, but I will never go back to that old man. Never!"

The family continued until they came to the church at the other end of the village. Rosario went into the chapel to talk to the priest, while Juana remained outside with the children. After an hour, Rosario came out and sat by Juana. The children were playing tag on the steps, running around the yard and into the cemetery, raising dust, yelling.

Rosario took the baby from Juana. Leaning against the wall of the church, she calmly watched the sunset begin over the village. Juana waited in silence.

"Outside the village, the priest says there is a convent. We will go there."

Suspicious, Juana watched Rosario. The look of serenity, like a mask, had hardened on Rosario's face. Juana said nothing, but began to gather the children for the long walk to the convent.

When I was a child, I believed that angels lived in churches. I was certain of this because when we went to church on Sundays, angels sat in the front pews with the children. They wore long white gowns that rustled with starch. Their haloes were made of stiff white fabric that framed their faces like wings. In His efficiency, God had combined their wings and haloes into one. He knew what He was doing.

I would always walk alone to the front of the church and quietly sit next to one of the angels. Furtively, I would study her dress. Angels did not wear wrinkled dresses. They had no hair either. I was fascinated by this. My hair was the bane of my life. It took too long for my mother to remove the tangles every morning. My ringlets were profuse, a heady temptation to every little boy who sat behind me in the classroom, or in the church pew. They would pull the ends of the curls and watch them spring back.

I lived to grind these little boys into the tarmac of the playground, and spent many recesses sitting at my desk in punishment for bloodying their noses, or knocking them nearly unconscious. I was never sorry for the punishments. They were worth every drop of blood I drew. The ones who pulled my hair in church I left alone until we crossed the parking lot behind the church on our way to catechism class. They seldom made it to the class.

Angels were special, both for their starched dresses and for *their lack of hair. They also smelled good, fresh and clean. Heaven must be like this, I thought.*

Sitting next to the nuns in church every Sunday was the closest I could get to heaven; I never prayed.

CHAPTER 9

"We can take only one child. We would like to help you with all of them, but we are a poor convent. We will barely be able to manage one."

The Mother Superior was a kindly looking woman. She felt sympathy as she watched Rosario sit before her desk and nurse her baby. Juana sat beside her and had not spoken since they had been ushered into the office. Instead, she had surveyed it carefully, noticing the highly polished hardwood floor, the spotless windows, the devastating neatness of the room.

Rosario turned to Juana.

"I will need Victorio and María to help me. I cannot leave the baby, of course. Eduardo would not stay here without the others. He would run away. Carlos still needs our care."

Juana stared in shock at Rosario as she quickly realized that Rosario was indeed contemplating leaving one of the children with the nuns. She did not move or speak. She waited.

"I will leave Pilar," Rosario said to the Mother Superior. "She is a very good little girl. And she is bright. She learns quickly. Will you teach her to read, Mother?"

The Mother Superior looked at Rosario and then

for her good.   similar to father

at Juana. Juana was rigid, anger turning her soft face to granite as she stared at Rosario.

"Yes. We will teach her. To read. To write. She will learn French. She will be taught to sew. We will take care of her for you."

"I have nothing to give you for her care."

"We will care for her as if you did, Rosario. She will be happy here."

Rosario rose from her chair and transferred the baby to her other arm and then buttoned her blouse.

"I must go now and say good-bye to Pilar."

"Rosario, I do not think that would be wise. I will explain to her after you have left."

Rosario looked at Juana, who was now staring out of the window, expressionless. Not certain what to do next, Rosario turned and left the room. The Mother Superior looked at Juana and waited.

Juana stood up and reached into the deep pocket of her skirt. From it she brought out a large leather purse. She opened it and removed the emeralds she had taken from Pilar's bedroom. Placing them on the desk in front of the Mother Superior, she looked directly into her eyes.

"We will return for Pilar. Tell her that."

During the years my Aunt Pilar was in the convent, thirteen years in fact, we do not know for certain what became of my grandmother and the rest of the children. My mother told me that her brother, Victorio, seldom spoke of those years. Neither did María. Eduardo apparently left for the agricultural fields of California before he was sixteen. Victorio related stories to his baby sister, Teresita, of the early mornings helping his mother and María make tamales to sell from the small wooden wagon he would pull around town. The first year the wagon was unpainted, but the following year, Victorio painted it blue. By selling the tamales every day, they survived and prospered enough eventually to own a restaurant in Hermosillo.

PART 3

CHAPTER 1

Sitting upon a low, brick wall within the gardens of the convent, Pilar liked to listen quietly. A silence, like warm cream, engulfed her; sounds were muffled, as if they came from a distant star. She could feel the earth sway beneath her, feel it breathe. As the days and weeks passed, she timed her rhythms to the passive beating of the convent's inner heart. The peace soothed her isolation and her sense of abandonment and soon she forgot the faces of her brothers and sisters. All that she could remember of her mother's face was the blue of her eyes; the eyes came to her in dreams. Pilar saw them on her embroidery linen as she sat with the nuns and practiced her stitches.

No one had spoken to her during the first year, except the Mother Superior, and Pilar seldom saw her. In fact, her fifth birthday had passed without anyone's knowledge, not even her own. She lost track of her age and ceased thinking about it as the days ran into one another and took on the color and ambience of the lemon groves surrounding the convent.

She played in the garden during the warmest hours of the afternoons when the nuns were sleeping. In the pond she created small boats of rose petals, floating them around the fountain like a small armada. Trailing like lifeboats were orange-blossom canoes, entwined and bobbing, drowning lovers in a little girl's fantasy. Because of the rule of silence, Pilar would sing softly, barely above a whisper, serenading her flower world, enchanting it to her will.

> *Au clair de la lune*
> *Mon ami Pierrot*
> *Prête-moi ta plume*
> *pour ecrire un mot . . .*

When Pilar was eight she accidently discovered a tiny hole in the garden wall. The flower she was attempting to pluck from its stem was brushing against a moss-covered brick. Pilar scratched her arm on it, for it was sticking out at an angle, waiting for many years to feel a small girl's touch. She rubbed her fingers against her forearm and examined the brick. She could see sunlight around its edges. Bending near to the wall she scraped it out of its niche. She looked behind her into the courtyard. The nuns were all asleep, the Mother Superior in her office.

Pilar began working the other bricks loose from around the edge of the hole, pulling on them slowly, the way she had worked on her front tooth last month. Another brick came loose. She looked around for a place to hide the bricks then realized it would be better to place them back in the wall so the nuns would not discover her secret. Carefully, she placed each brick on the other side of the hole until she had enough removed so she could wriggle through. She turned around and replaced each brick. Then, she was free.

The lemon grove was in full blossom and she explored it until she came to a large tree almost in the center of the seemingly endless rows. Climbing it carefully, branch by unsteady branch, she sat on the uppermost limb and made herself a crown of lemon blossoms. Pretending to be a bride of Christ, she remembered the final vows the novitiates had sworn at Christmas Mass. They dressed as brides in white lace gowns and veils, and at the end of the ceremony they donned their new habits after having all their beautiful hair cut off. Pilar didn't like that part of the ceremony. She could not understand the joy on the novitiates' faces as their heads were shaved. She reached up and patted her lemon blossoms and entwined some more of them into her long black hair. She had no intention of letting anyone cut off her hair. The nuns would braid it every morning, but by noon Pilar would have it undone and hanging down her back. It rippled in waves and comforted her. She didn't like it braided.

She fell asleep in the tree, her arms wrapped around the branches, her face against the trunk. When she awoke, the sun was halfway down the sky. She scrambled from the tree and ran back to the brick wall. After she had replaced each brick, she returned to the pond. The nuns were emerging from their cells and hurrying to resume their afternoon labors. Pilar realized she had not been missed.

There was now a new element in her life. The restraints of the convent would be easier to bear, for every day during the siesta she could escape to her lemon grove. That night her sleep was undisturbed. There were no nightmares of thirst or hunger or snakes. Now she woke each morning full of anticipation.

CHAPTER 2

1922

Pilar woke with a current of pain in her body. Waves of pain, like seawater tearing at a lonely beach, bathed her from neck to ankles. She tried to sit up, but the painful throbbing in her head stopped her. She lay there, the sun beating down on her, and tried to remember what had happened. She remembered the man reaching for her as she walked through the lemon grove. She remembered him hitting her when she tried to get away. She remembered . . . what?

She lifted her arm; her shoulder ached. As she sat up, dizziness washed over her, so she steadied herself with her hands. Suddenly, she felt what seemed to be a liquid of some sort on her leg. She looked down to see an opaque and blood-streaked substance. She touched it. It felt sticky. When she tried to stand, she was struck with an agonizing pain in her abdomen. It doubled her over and she collapsed back to the ground. She didn't move, waiting for it to pass, but it didn't. Instead, it leveled to a dull, burning sensation. Total exhaustion flooded her body and mind. She began to notice her arms and legs were scratched. The backs of them were embedded with small particles of dirt and sand. She tried to brush them off, but many smaller pieces remained, stinging her anew. The fluid between her legs continued to seep out, sticky and uncomfortable. It smelled strange, different. She didn't like it.

She tried to get up again, and this time succeeded. There was no one around. She wasn't certain where she was, but in the distance she recognized the bell tower of the convent chapel. The sun was low in the sky, but it was still hot and humid. She knew she had to get back to the convent, but when she began to walk the stickiness was so uncomfortable that she paused and looked around for something to wipe herself with. There were only bushes with few leaves, so she used her dress.

She began walking in the direction of the convent wall. She didn't know why, but she knew she didn't want anyone to see her. She must get back quickly and change her dress. As she walked, the ache in her stomach became worse. She knew she was bleeding. Where was the man who pulled her to the edge of the lemon grove? She quickened her pace, frightened he would find her again.

She entered through the wall of the garden and went immediately into her cell. The nuns were still napping. She carefully removed her other dress from its hook on the wall and laid it on the bed. As she undressed she noticed the inside of her legs were streaked with the opaque, bloody fluid. Again, she looked for something to wipe her legs with, but could find nothing the nuns wouldn't see later. Quietly, she went out through the garden to the pond and began to wash herself. When she was finished, she returned to the cell, dried herself with her dress, and rolled the soiled garment into a ball. She put on her other dress, went back to the pond, and began to dig a hole behind Sister María's roses. The dirt broke some of her fingernails, but she didn't care. She was desperate to dig the hole deep enough so that no one would ever find her dress. She found a stick to help break up the claylike soil. Finally, the hole was deep enough. She threw the dress in and began pushing the dirt on top of it.

With each handful she exchanged her memory of the day for a reality filled with denial. She packed down the dirt the way she had seen Sister Filomena do when she buried the garbage. She brushed off her hands and then her dress. It was almost time for the nuns to waken. She went back into her cell and cleaned up and dried the floor, then she made certain everything was in order. As she came out of the cell she heard the nuns entering the garden. Ignoring her pain as best she could, she went to join them.

Pilar did not leave the convent again, and soon she forgot the loose bricks. She forgot the man, and the blood, and the pain. The fear was the only thing she did not forget.

In 1949, my father bought a ranch in Central California. It is a piece of property that runs along the ridge of the Stanislaus River above Angel's Camp. The entrance is hidden in a grove of scrub oaks. If you go there, you need to know exactly where the entrance is located.

As you enter the ranch there is a wild pear tree to the left of the main gate. It blooms every April and drops its white blossoms like blessings on all who enter. There are wildflowers growing on the hill that do not grow anywhere else in the area.

In midsummer the ranch is dry. The leaves shrivel and fall off the fig trees that grow in the valley below the entrance. The olive trees my paternal grandfather planted at the right of the entrance turn silver; their leaves rise in awe toward the sunlight. My grandfather walked and dreamed there, and it is where he is buried now.

My parents lived on the ranch in 1950 when I was born, and my grandfather came to live with us. He and my Grandmother Isobel had separated in their old age. Isobel remained at the family's home in Santa Barbara.

My mother had never heard the gypsy siguiriya, but she heard it the day my grandfather arrived and every morning until he died. Since he seldom left my side when I was an infant, my earliest memory is of the sound and essence of the gypsy siguiriya. It is a mournful, nostalgic chanting; a song of loss lifted from the heart and offered to an indifferent sky.

It is the chanting of my grandfather's Egyptian forebears, carried forward through generations and brought north to Spain in his family's Moslem rituals. My grandfather, Salvador, began and ended our day singing this song, accompanying himself with a guitar.

I remember waking in the night and seeing him asleep in a kitchen chair propped against my crib. He took long walks on the ranch carrying me, and when I could walk, he held my hand. He believed in magic and all things metaphysical and would talk to me about them in a combination of Castilian and broken English.

He had been in the military as a young man in Spain, and still had his very old and very long rifle. Often he would walk from the ranch to Yosemite to shoot a deer, then carry it back on his shoulders to the ranch. He would be gone for days, but on his return he would dress out the deer, hang it in the cellar, and thus provide for himself. Every day I waited at the entrance of the ranch for him to return, falling asleep under the olive trees.

I have had a continuous dream most of my life about my grandfather and this time of our lives. Actually, it is a recurring nightmare. When I was grown, I told my mother about it. She was amazed that I remembered and told me the story behind my dream.

I was toddling behind her as she carried a basket of laundry to the clothesline that stood beside the kitchen door. My grandfather had just finished cleaning his rifle when he saw the snake. It was beside the path we were following. My grandfather later said I must have heard its rattles when he did, because he was aware of me suddenly stopping and staring at something. I was between him and the snake and it was coiled and ready to strike. He shot it and its head ex-

ploded all over me. In my dreams, I feel the warmth of the
sunlight, hear the buzzing of the insects in the grass, and see
the snake's eyes through the blinding glare of that light. I
was two years old.

My grandfather must have considered, in the few seconds
he had to consider anything, that his shot could very well
have killed me. Later, in the midst of her gratitude, my
mother realized this too. She confronted him and he replied,

"Better I would have killed her in love than the snake
kill her in evil."

I am unable to return to the ranch now as often as I
would like. It is my garden of make-believe. It is home,
where the pear blossoms bless me again, and in my memories I am taken back to the entrance and I am four. My
grandfather is walking down the road toward the gate carrying a deer on his shoulders. His smile is full of a simple
love, and I know now that I was his homecoming, a part of
Spain he believed he had lost only to find it again in a
touch of my cheek. It was a healing touch that placed me in
a state of grace, forever suspending me somewhere between
the senses and emotions.

PART 4

CHAPTER 1

1928—Hermosillo

Victorio Pérez unlocked the door to the restaurant. It was dark inside, but he did not turn on the light. The sun would begin to rise in the next few moments so he instinctively made his way through the small dining area and into the kitchen in back. He took the broom from the closet and began sweeping the kitchen floor. He wanted to have it clean before his wife, Jimena, arrived to begin the cooking.

She entered with their two oldest children, five-year-old Inez and four-year-old Ana. Without being told, the little girls began placing the chairs on the tables so Victorio could sweep the dining room floor. His wife went into the kitchen to begin cooking breakfast for the early customers who would arrive with the sunlight.

" 'Torio, what time do you leave to go to the convent?"

"As soon as we are finished serving lunch."

"Rosario is anxious about Pilar coming home. She was very nervous this morning when I left the baby with her and Juana."

Jimena continued cooking while she talked. She and Victorio had been married six years. He had been sixteen, and Jimena barely thirteen. They had opened the restaurant every morning since the day after their wedding. María and her husband, Juan, arrived at noon to help Rosario with the cooking for the dinner crowd, and fourteen-year-old Juanita took the dinner orders. Eduardo had left Hermosillo four years earlier, beckoned by the promises of work in the fields of Southern California. Carlos had recently followed, but after a year he returned, lonely for his family, bringing with him his young new wife. Her father, a Portuguese farmer, had owned the ranch where Carlos worked, and when Carlos left to return home, Catarina had eloped with him, leaving her twin sister to their parent's wrath.

Unknown to Carlos, Catarina could not cook. This incredible failing in the Pérez family was discovered one morning when Catarina, wanting to become a member of the family in spirit also, offered to cook the beans for the restaurant. She took the dry pinto beans and poured them into a frying pan. She lit the fire under the pan and stirred the beans, adding salt. She continued to stir as the beans began to burn.

Rosario watched Catarina in disbelief. The smell of scorched beans brought the rest of the family from their chores. They began laughing until tears formed in the corners of their eyes. Catarina turned to them, smoke engulfing her from the pan, and burst out crying. Filled with pity, Rosario took the sobbing girl into her arms while furtively turning off the fire under the pan.

She waved the rest of the children out of the kitchen, calmed Catarina, and began her first lessons in cooking. Within a year, Catarina would be the only one allowed to help Rosario make the tamales for which the restaurant was famous. It was Catarina who devised the most delicious moles and sauces, but the legend of the beans would plague her the rest of her life.

CHAPTER 2

Victorio harnessed the family's horse to the wagon and left for the convent. The sun was high. He knew it would be nearly sundown before he returned with Pilar.

He arrived at the convent and rang the bell outside the gate. A nun approached silently, appearing to float toward the entrance.

"I have come for my sister, Pilar. I am Victorio Pérez."

"Yes, Señor Pérez. Please, will you wait there, and I will inform the Mother Superior."

She glided through the small inner courtyard and disappeared through the archway. Victorio waited, surveying the walls of the convent. They were white-washed and blinding with the sun's reflection. He moved to the left, into some shade, and waited for Pilar. He had not seen her since Rosario left her there thirteen years ago. Juana and Rosario had visited Pilar twice, when they could afford to leave the struggling restaurant, but since the family had enlarged with wives and grandchildren, Rosario had been unable to visit. Juana had weakened in her later years, unable to help Rosario except with the grandchildren. When Rosario and Juana had visited last, Pilar was eleven.

He heard footsteps and looking toward the arch, he saw the Mother Superior, her black habit moving

softly about her as she led Pilar through the courtyard
and into the glaring sunlight. The young woman was
carrying a small valise. Victorio watched Pilar in
amazement as the nun put her arms around her and
held her for a moment. She whispered something in
Pilar's ear and then released her.

Victorio stared at Pilar as she approached the gate.
His sister, María, had never lost her childhood soft-
ness, and with the birth of her first child, Irena, she
had held onto her fat as if it were to be treasured. She
was a clumsy young woman who spilled food onto
the restaurant floor. They always knew where she was
from the constant noise she made.

Juanita, at fourteen, was a chatterbox, always talking and sometimes making pointed and caustic remarks, especially about men. Victorio tried not to
listen to her. His wife, Jimena, was a gentle, quiet
creature, nearly invisible in the kitchen. All his life he
would envision Jimena in front of a stove. He was not
at all prepared for Pilar.

Her white cotton dress was embroidered down to
its floor-length hem in white silk threads that glistened and reflected the sunlight. From his place in the
shade, Pilar appeared to glow. The light collided with
her blue-black hair causing sparks to burst about her
head. She was tall and too slender. She appeared to
have little substance, until he looked into her eyes.
They were the color of turquoise. No, that wasn't
right. They were a pale, greenish blue. No. They
were like crystals. That was better. He could see into
them. He did not realize until six years later when he
would see the ocean for the first time that looking

into Pilar's eyes was like tumbling into cool, crystal-line waters. For the rest of his life he would be filled with guilt at the sight of the ocean. But now, unaware of what was to come, he walked up to his sister and held out his hand.

"I am your brother, Victorio. You may not remember me. You were so little when Mamá brought you here. I have come to take you home."

Not moving, except to place her hand in his, Pilar answered him softly.

"I remember you, 'Torio. You carried me through the mountains. My feet were bleeding. You placed me on the floor of the chapel, before the Virgin."

Victorio could only stare at her, and then, in awkward embarrassment, he led her to the cart, helping her onto the seat and placing her valise in the back. They did not speak more than a few words, commenting only on the countryside as they journeyed home. When they arrived at their mother's house, Victorio was in a quandary about what to do with this beautiful creature beside him.

Pilar existed in a private world. She had begun creating it soon after her arrival at the convent. She insulated herself within it and was happy. Leaving the convent now had caused a shock to her psyche that she did not understand. Victorio was her brother, but the only man she had seen for thirteen years was the priest who said Mass at the convent and heard her confession. Sitting next to Victorio now made her feel extremely self-conscious. She did not know what to say to him. She was not used to talking because of the rule of silence observed in the convent. She was content with her own thoughts and company, for over the years she had become her own best friend. This aloofness gave her an inner strength that would forever set her apart from her brothers and sisters.

She appeared elegant and serene, but beneath this unintentional facade was a shyness that would overwhelm her for her entire life. She could not connect, relate, or even emotionally touch another person. When finally this would happen, both of the people involved would be cruelly torn away from her. For now, though, she was in awe of the countryside about her. She was away from the convent, her life was just beginning, and this was her older brother, Victorio, come to take her home to her mother, to Juana, and to her brothers and sisters. Already, despite her discomfort, she adored Victorio.

CHAPTER 3

Rosario's house was built on a dusty street and looked as if it were sinking into the ground. Of white adobe, it had a small, worn wooden porch in front. There was also a low step that Pilar hardly noticed as she approached the door. When she entered, she could not immediately see. She stood in the middle of the doorway, outlined in the late-afternoon light, waiting for her eyes to adjust. The family inside could not see her face until Victorio filled the space around her as he stepped in behind Pilar.

Rosario rushed forward and embraced her. Tears were flowing freely down her cheeks as she turned toward the rest of the children and presented their sister.

Carlos hesitantly walked up to Pilar and stood in front of her, embarrassed. He knew he was not attractive, and felt certain his sister would reject him. Pilar reached out, and with a healing touch, placed her hand on Carlos's cheek.

"Carlos, I have missed you so much. I am so glad you healed so well from the snake." In a whisper, she continued.

"I know I saw a miracle that day, when your fever finally broke and you opened your eyes and looked at me. We had all prayed for it."

Like a man in a dream, Carlos walked into his sister's arms. He began crying as he told her how much he had looked forward to the day she would come home.

"Now you are here, and we are together again." He turned to Catarina.

"This is my wife, Catarina, and this is my son, Little 'Torio."

Catarina approached Pilar and placed the baby in her arms. The rest of the family rushed forward and began embracing her. There was much laughing and crying. In the midst of the confusion and joy, Juana entered the room from the kitchen. She was wiping her hands on the apron she always wore. Pilar saw her first and became very still. Her silence caused the rest of the family to move away from her as Juana approached. In her old age and senility she believed she was seeing her mistress again. She embraced Pilar.

"Señora, you have come back to us. We have waited so long. At last you are here."

She took Pilar's face in her hands and kissed her on each cheek. Pilar, not understanding, but sensing she was someone else to Juana, replied,

"Yes, I have come home, Juana. I will not leave again."

Juana's face filled with a joyous light. She turned to the rest of the family and said,

"Let us sit now. The food is ready. We will have our feast."

They all moved together into the large kitchen and began seating themselves and their children around the table in a noisy, laughing group, while Victorio remained for a moment in the parlor, perplexed and bewildered. He placed Pilar's valise on the floor and turned to close the front door. The sun was nearly gone now, and only the faint stars gave evidence to the existence of more than the lives of his family. He sighed heavily, then joined them in the kitchen.

My mother, Teresita, seldom cooked Mexican food. She didn't know how. Having so many older sisters who had cooked for the family restaurant during their younger years, it was never necessary for her to learn. As the baby of the family, she simply sat down and the food was placed in front of her. This did not change while I was a child, and it still has not changed today. I can go to my Aunt Juanita's, sit at her kitchen table, and she will feed me. The food is always ready. When I walk through the back door of her house the wonderful odors of tamales, sopa, refried beans, and fresh tortillas embrace me in a warm, steamy cloud.

Her sopa is made with tomatoes, onions, garlic, and vermicelli crumbled before it is cooked in this aromatic mixture. It is soupy and thick, and as I eat it, I know again the securities of my childhood.

Once, when I was in my early twenties, my mother and I decided to make tamales. We found a recipe in one of my cookbooks and carefully followed it. The masa was in a bowl, looking like a voluminous, flour-sack pillow. We soaked a huge pile of corn husks and carefully made the filling. As an afterthought, we added raisins to it. We began forming each tamale carefully, wrapping it in corn husks and tying it with strips of the husks the way the book instructed. We went about this seriously . . . for a while.

The masa seemed to grow the more we took from the bowl. It had babies. We formed about thirty tamales, and still the bowl was half full. The sun was going down. We had invited friends and relatives for our tamale dinner. They would be arriving shortly and the kitchen was still full of masa. I picked up a handful of masa (I had discarded the large spoon about ten tamales back) and tossed it at the corn husk in my other hand. I had developed a dead aim. I tossed some filling on it and then some more masa. I wrapped it, tied it, and threw it across the room. It missed the steamer.

"Whoops, Mom. I dropped one of yours on the floor."

My mother turned in time to see me throw some more masa at the new corn husk in my hand. It missed. She began to giggle. I picked up the masa from the floor and threw it in the sink, but I missed again and instead hit her on the back of the leg. She scraped it off and threw it back at me. The fight was on.

When the guests arrived, we were in the kitchen, both covered with masa. I had stuck some corn husks in my hair and on my mother's nose. We were giggling hysterically, sitting on the floor, throwing mounds of masa at corn husks, tying them together any old way, and tossing them into the steamer. We had nearly four dozen, all shapes and sizes, some of the husks oozing masa, and some missing the filling. These were the "surprise" tamales.

My Aunt Juanita and Aunt Pilar came into the house through the kitchen door. They stared at us in shock and gave each other a hopeless look. They began cleaning up the mess while my mother and I continued sitting on the floor, laughing uncontrollably and smearing each other with masa. I have never made tamales since, neither has my mother.

CHAPTER 4

After thirteen years of hardship and struggle, of meeting challenges and prevailing against them, Rosario's family was stymied by what to do with Pilar. She could not cook. She had never done any manual labor while in the convent. Her talents were in her fingers. She could make lace. Her embroidery stitches were perfectly executed. She could look at a dress and after eyeing it a few moments, cut a pattern freehand. The dresses she made for women in the family fit them perfectly. Catarina suggested that Pilar could make dresses for the other women of the village, but she forgot, until Juanita reminded her, that the other women were as poor, or poorer, than they were. There was no market for Pilar's creations.

She asked to work in the restaurant, but Victorio could not find a job suitable for her inabilities until one evening he suggested she take dinner orders from the customers.

The tiny restaurant was noisy that night, as was usual for Saturday evening, but suddenly there was silence. Victorio didn't realize it at first. He continued helping Jimena and his mother with the cooking. He was so engrossed in what he was doing, that Rosario had to shake his arm to get his attention. He turned to her. Rosario's eyes were large and questioning. He saw that Jimena was staring at the swinging door that led from the kitchen to the dining area. The silence engulfed them.

Hesitantly, Victorio approached the door and looked through the small window. Everything appeared to be in order. Pilar was standing next to a table speaking to a customer who was looking at his plate and nodding his head up and down. Victorio entered the dining room and saw that most of the men were staring at Pilar in silence. The rest were looking at each other in bewilderment. As Victorio approached the table she was serving, he heard her speaking to the man, who was still staring at his plate.

"And what would you like to drink with your meal, Señor?"

With a respect Victorio had never seen from any of his friends and customers, the man replied, "A beer would be fine, Señorita, thank you."

"All right, Señor."

Pilar turned toward another table and the couple sitting there began staring at their plates. Victorio then realized that, without meaning to, Pilar was intimidating the customers. Quickly, he went to Pilar and gently taking her notepad from her hand he said,

"Pilar, Mamá and Jimena need your help in the kitchen. I will take the orders for you."

Obediently, Pilar went into the kitchen. There drifted through the room a soft, collective sigh. The customers began speaking to one another as the air again filled with their noise. With relief, Victorio turned to his customer.

Later that night, after the family had gone to bed, Victorio sat up with Rosario. Both were in a quandary. They loved Pilar, but they also realized she was not suited for any kind of work they could offer her. She helped with the grandchildren, but Juana had been managing them well since they were born—she didn't really need Pilar's help.

"Mamá, we need to think of something. We cannot just leave Pilar to whatever fate brings to her."

"I know, 'Torio, but what can we do? She is only suited for the convent. She does not want to become a nun. That is why we brought her home. She should be married."

"Married? Whom shall we have her marry, Mamá? Reuben? How about Reuben? She can work in his fields. Pick his beans. Live in that shack of his. Is that what we want for her? She will die like that, Mamá! Who is there in this village for her to marry?"

"There is no one, 'Torio. I know that. I have thought about this so much. Worried about it. I do not know the answer."

Victorio got up from his chair and walked across the room to his mother. Kneeling in front of her, he embraced her.

"Do not worry. We will find the answer. Pilar must be happy, more than anything else, she will be happy. I promise you that. We will give it time. It will work out, Mamá."

The following night the restaurant was closed. It was Sunday, the family's one night off. They were sitting at the kitchen table having dinner when there was a knock at the front door. Victorio went to answer it. Standing there was his brother, Eduardo. They ecstatically embraced each other. The rest of the family rushed into the parlor, crowding around Eduardo. They had not seen him in six years and he was huskier and taller than they remembered. He brought gifts for everyone. They sat him at the table and began feeding him.

"Eduardo, tell us about California. Did you like it there?"

"Yes, Mamá. It is a beautiful country, up north. Everything is green. It is not dry and dusty like this. There is work for everyone, and money too. Look."

He reached into his pockets and began emptying them onto the table. American currency, in tens and twenties, floated down to the cotton cloth. Scooping it up, he offered it to his mother.

"Here, for you, Mamá."

Rosario stared at the bills in his hand, and looked at Victorio. He was stunned.

"Where did you get this money, Eduardo? Did you steal it?" he asked sternly.

Laughing, Eduardo answered, "No, 'Torio. I did not steal it. I earned it. I worked in the harvest in San Joaquin Valley, then I traveled to Los Angeles to pick oranges. There is a lot of work in California. A lot of money to be earned."

Victorio picked up the bills from the table where Rosario had dropped them.

"Everybody works in California, Eduardo?"

"Well, yes. I guess if they want to, everybody works. I will return in a week. It is almost time to pick the lettuce again in Salinas."

"It is good to have you home again, Eduardo," Victorio said. "Jimena, put the children to bed. It is late. I want to talk to my brother. Everyone should go to bed now."

Without questioning Victorio's authority, they all left and he and Eduardo stayed up very late that night talking about California.

After his brother left to return North, Victorio had one goal in mind—to move his entire family to California. He meant to do this as soon as he could save enough money from the restaurant. It would take a long time, for their profit was small and barely enough to take care of their needs, but Victorio was determined to take his family to a better life. He became even more resolute as he realized the answer to Pilar's future might be found in California.

Eduardo, however, would forever remain elusive, returning after months or years. Telling stories of his travels, his eyes would lovingly follow Rosario as she walked back and forth from the stove, serving the family as they listened intently to Eduardo's adventures. His adoration of his mother never wavered, and he demonstrated his devotion with the money he brought or sent to her. Eduardo lived the life of a migrant worker, his existence permeated by loneliness. He never married, but traveled the length of California, following the crops, sharing living quarters with other workers. He never told his family of his endless despair, and he managed adroitly to hide his alcoholism from them. He died alone, of cirrhosis, in the San Joaquin County Hospital ward three years after Rosario's death. Victorio learned of his brother's death after being notified by the hospital, as Eduardo had listed him as next of kin. Victorio buried his brother next to Rosario.

Grandmother Rosario's house in Santa Barbara was very small. I was fascinated with it. All the rooms were diminutive, and the floors were covered with linoleum, even the living room. This especially intrigued me. It was a narrow house with two bedrooms separated by a tiny bathroom. As you entered the front door, you stepped into the living room. On the right, my grandmother had placed a bed. It was narrow, with an iron frame and headboard. Though there were two bedrooms, Rosario slept in the bed in the living room. This long room continued to the back of the house and became the kitchen. My family went often to see my grandmother, but in my memories, I don't recall where each of us sat during these visits. I only remember that I would sit in a chair across from the bed and watch Rosario.

Her hair was a glistening, silver-white. She wore it in a coiled braid, secured at the nape of her neck. At night, she would sit on her bed and unwind the braid, slowly loosening it, running her fingers through the plaits until they were separated. Her hair would hang over her shoulder and down the front of her chest. It was straight and shiny. I, with my abundance of unruly curls, was fascinated by her hair. She would begin to brush it with rhythmic strokes, starting from the top of her head and drawing the brush all the way to the ends, slowly, ritualistically, and she would begin to rock back and forth.

Within a few moments the chanting would begin. It

started almost in a whisper, as if she were singing to herself. In a French and Spanish dialect, she would begin to recite the names of our ancestors, and slowly the atmosphere began to change until I could feel them around me. She was taught to recite her lineage by her mother, who had been taught by her mother, who had learned from her mother, on and on, all the way back to the Mayan pyramids. It took my grandmother over an hour to recite all the names.

Mesmerized by the sound of her singing, entranced by the slow brushing of her hair, the rocking of her body, I would be lifted out of my small world to a place full of magic. She did this only at night, and I remember it now with grief for something irretrievable. The chant was lost to us when her sudden illness overtook her. In the confusion of caring for her in her final days, none of her children thought to make this record. Our Mayan heritage was lost forever, and all that I can pass of it to my children are my memories of a tiny room, dimly lighted, my grandmother sitting on her bed brushing her silver hair, rocking, singing the melody of our ancestors. We had taken for granted an oral tradition that had been in place for generations. Someone was going to learn it someday. If it had been saved I could take down my hair and sing my grandmother's song for you.

CHAPTER 5

1928—Hermosillo

Rosario was in the kitchen making chocolate when Pilar entered the room. She sat at the table and stared blankly at the white tablecloth. The grandchildren would not be coming to stay for the day. Catarina was home with Little Victorio, and Jimena, in the fourth month of her pregnancy, was home still suffering from morning sickness. She could not abide the sight of food, and so would not be working in the restaurant until after the baby was born. This left Pilar, who had been helping watch the children, with time on her hands.

"Mamá, is there something I could do to help you today?"

Rosario poured Pilar a cup of chocolate and sat at the table with her. Pilar made an effort to be cheerful, but Rosario was aware of her daughter's restlessness. Before she could respond to her, Juanita came bouncing into the room.

"Is there chocolate left for me, Mamá? Where are the rolls? Did Victorio go out to get some this morning, or did he run off to the restaurant?"

She sat down heavily in one of the kitchen chairs, spilling her drink onto the tablecloth. It puddled briefly on the starched cloth and then slowly began to seep in. Rosario immediately started the mopping ritual she had performed since Juanita began to walk.

"Oops, sorry, Mamá. Morning, Pilar."

Juanita propped her chin on her hand and stared at Pilar. Her sister was immaculate this morning. How did she accomplish this? Juanita could not fathom Pilar. Her dresses were always pristine, even when she was chasing those brats around. Her hair was shiny and clean, every strand in place. The heat never seemed to bother her. Didn't she sweat?

"Mamá, where are the children?"

"They are with their mothers this morning. Juanita, will you stop spilling that chocolate? You are ruining my tablecloth!"

"I don't know, Mamá. Jimena is pregnant again, and she is still carrying the baby around in her arms. I don't understand Victorio, or men for that matter. He will bury himself with his—"

"Juanita! Be quiet."

Pilar looked from her sister to her mother. By now, she was used to Juanita's blunt remarks. She understood her sister's nature, even if she didn't always understand what she was talking about. While the rest of the family was constantly shocked by Juanita's observations, Pilar loved and appreciated her sister's candidness. She understood that not a part of Juanita was vicious or mean. She simply said what she thought while living in the midst of a family that painfully avoided personal issues. This candidness was almost a necessity when everyone's lives intertwined so tightly. There was no privacy other than what they could preserve for themselves, and always it was hard won.

Pilar understood that Juanita dealt with her own loss of privacy by invading everyone else's.

"Pilar, there is an errand you could run for me this morning. Victorio said we are low on rice at the restaurant. With Jimena not there to help him, he cannot go to Calderón's store to get some more. Will you walk over there and ask Señor Calderón's son to deliver one hundred pounds to the restaurant this afternoon?"

"Yes, Mamá. Of course. I will leave right now."

Pilar picked up her shawl, threw it around her shoulders and left the house. Rosario gave Juanita a stern look. Juanita shrugged her shoulders and finished her chocolate.

The air was already beginning to warm, though it was not yet nine o'clock. Pilar spent most of her time in the house with the children, so it was a special source of joy to be sent on an errand by her mother. As she approached Calderón's store, she did not notice Gabriel Calderón in the upper window of the building. He kept his office there so he could oversee his many holdings in the town. His son, Eugenio, managed the store for him now. His other son, Christino, managed most of the other businesses, and Gabriel, in semiretirement though he was only forty-nine, spent his days overseeing them. This morning he was going over the books of the store. He was pleased with his oldest son's management; their profits were steadily increasing.

The air in Gabriel's office was becoming stale, so he had risen from the desk to open the window. He saw Pilar as she approached the store. He could only stare at her, his hand still on the window latch. He had not see a girl like this, certainly not in this village. Who was she?

She walked as if held by an invisible string, lightly, delicately. Her body gave the impression of total relaxation and ease. She was devoid of self-consciousness, comfortable with herself, confident. She is too young to be that confident, Gabriel thought. How old is she?

Her hair must never have been cut. It fell below her waist. The color of it reminded him of his favorite stallion. Black to where it was almost purple, it moved as if it were all of a piece. A cascade of hair.

Where did she come from? She disappeared from his view as she entered the store. Gabriel didn't realize he had been holding his breath until he suddenly exhaled. He carefully unlatched the window and threw it open. He breathed in deeply and tried to clear his head. He sat at the desk, looked at the ledgers, and then returned to the window to wait.

Presently, Pilar left the building and began walking back to her mother's house. Gabriel watched her until she disappeared from his view again. He stubbed out his cigar and went downstairs. Calling greetings to the customers, he made his way behind the counter. His son was helping another customer, so Gabriel was able to examine the orders Eugenio had taken so far that morning. Pilar's was on top. He read the name of the Pérez restaurant, and saw Pilar's signature on the order for one hundred pounds of rice. Breathing a sigh of relief, he returned to his office upstairs.

I was eleven years old when I began to overhear my parents discuss the plans for my marriage. I was bewildered. My father's voice never rose above its calm, quiet cadence. My mother's would become shrill and desperate. But once, I heard her say in a deadly, calm voice,

"Amparo will marry the man she loves, the man she chooses for herself. That is the way it will be!"

Since the age of seven, I had been sent every Saturday morning to my paternal Grandmother Isobel's. She lived in a large white Victorian in a stately old section of Santa Barbara. The house rambled and sprawled over its lawns and was surrounded by my grandmother's passion—bushes and climbing vines. There was a well-kept lawn in front of the house, but the rest of the yard was a jungle of Isobel's prolific planting. There were doors everywhere. Four led out to the veranda that surrounded two-thirds of the structure. The back door led into a large service porch and the massive kitchen where Isobel taught me to cook at her old-fashioned, wood-burning stove.

In the dining room, which was often flooded by sunlight from the wall of mullioned windows, she taught me my embroidery, making me repeatedly rip out my sloppy, crooked stitches. My hair would get in my face, in my mouth, itch down my neck as I sat in the radiated heat from the windows and labored over the linen napkins. I hated the lessons,

*but because she was so loving, and determined, I obediently
followed my grandmother's instructions.*

Isobel had a neighbor. Her neighbor had come from Eng-
land forty years earlier and spoke with traces of a clipped ac-
cent. My grandmother, on the other hand, spoke a very
broken English. One day, I was sitting on the veranda when
I overheard my grandmother talking to the neighbor.

"Good morning, Isobel. How are you this morning?"

"Good morning, Bayahtreece."

I muffled a giggle and eavesdropped as she talked to
Beatrice.

"Isobel, do you intend to clip that bush behind you? It
blocks the light to my dining room. We find it most un-
pleasant."

"No. I doan inten to treem it."

"Well, I think it is most uncooperative and unneighborly
of you. Don't you think your son would agree?"

"He does not care about my booshes, Bayahtreece."

"Well, perhaps if I have Harvey speak to him about the
vegetation about your property, maybe we could have something done about it. It is unseemly, Isobel. Surely you realize that."

I was on the floor of the veranda, trying desperately to
hush my laughter. I knew my grandmother heard me. I
waited, anticipating her reply. I could tell by the growing re-
serve in her voice, that she was irritated with Beatrice.

There was a long pause. I thought, oh boy, oh boy, here
it comes. I was well rewarded.

"You know one schetta? And another schetta on top?"

I peeked around the corner of the porch and saw Grandmother piling imaginary cow patties onto the palms of her
hands.

"*And another schetta on top?*"

At this point Isobel offered her two hands, holding the imaginary patties, to the shocked Beatrice.

"*For you, bad lady!*"

I climbed onto the wicker sofa on the porch in time to muffle my laughter with the chintz-covered pillows. My grandmother had done it to her again. Gotten into a row with much-burdened Beatrice. Eight-hundred years of stuck-up Spanish aristocracy had prevailed again.

Isobel returned to the house, via the veranda, where she took me by the ear and led me into the living room, again to lecture me sternly about the evils of listening to grown-ups' conversations.

When she would get mad at me like this I wanted to tell her that I would rather have been home playing with my brothers and the boys in the neighborhood. But I didn't. Instead, I labored over those stitches, and learned the basics of European cooking. I didn't appreciate what I was being taught, but I sensed my grandmother had her reasons. I never suspected I was being groomed for the marriage she and my father had arranged for me when I was three months old. I was to be sent to Spain when I reached my twelfth birthday, to live with the family of my chosen fiance until the age of sixteen, when I would be married to their son.

CHAPTER 6

Gabriel Calderón was a man in his middle years afflicted by love. He started having his lunch at the Pérez restaurant, hopefully waiting for a glimpse of Pilar. The entire family worked in the restaurant, so where was she? He couldn't ask. He was a married man with children older than Pilar. Gabriel's wife was obsessed with their children and two small grandchildren, but their marriage had turned into a relationship of convenience over ten years ago. He provided well for his family by working hard all his life. He had been content, if not periodically restless. But it was a restlessness he seldom questioned, and if he had, he would not have understood it anyway. So, he plodded on, overseeing the family businesses, placating his now ill wife, not expecting anything better for himself.

But now, there was Pilar. He had never felt this way. His wife was chosen for him, and being an obedient son he had married her. He did not expect love, only a negotiated peace, which he and Hermelina had established early in their marriage.

He began to search for Pilar around the village. She was nowhere to be found. Finally in frustration, Gabriel approached Victorio late one evening as he was about to close the restaurant.

"Victorio, I would like to talk to you. In private, if possible."

"Oh, hello, Señor Calderón. Yes, of course, in private. What can I do for you, sir?"

Respectfully, Victorio led Gabriel back into the restaurant. He took him behind the kitchen into the small office he had made for himself. Often when he needed privacy, this was the only place he could go. They sat down, Victorio waited respectfully. Señor Calderón was an important man in their small community. Everyone treated him with respect.

"Victorio, this is very difficult for me. I don't know quite how to say this to you."

"Señor Calderón, please feel free to discuss anything with me. I am here to serve you, sir."

"Yes, well, you see. It is about your sister."

"My sister? Juanita? Has she said something? I am so sorry, Señor Calderón. She has no respect. She says what she wants and does not consider the effect. Has she offended you? I will speak to her. Tell me what she has said."

"No, no. Not Juanita. Juanita is a good girl. A bit bold, perhaps. Honest, actually. But this is not about Juanita."

Victorio was puzzled.

"Not Juanita?"

"No. You see. I mean to talk to you about another sister."

Victorio waited. The silence deepened as Gabriel tried to find words that would not offend Victorio. Somehow he knew that this moment was critical to his life and his well-being. He was driven by emotions he did not understand. Since being married he had been in control of everything in his life—his wife, his family, his business. Now, sitting in front of Victorio, Gabriel slowly surrendered that control.

"It is your sister, Pilar, I wish to talk to you about."

Victorio looked at Gabriel, a closed expression on his face, and did not reply. Gabriel waited a few seconds, then began again.

"This is most difficult, Victorio. I know I am in no position to inquire about your sister, my being a married man with a family. Children, in fact, older than Pilar. A wife. Yes, of course. A wife. . . ."

Victorio continued to wait silently. He suspected what Gabriel wanted, but he was not going to help him by offering his immediate understanding. There was something to be gained here, but Victorio did not yet know what it was.

Gabriel continued, losing more control, giving it over to Victorio as one transfers power long held and wearied by it.

"Your sister, with respect, Victorio, is a very beautiful young woman."

He paused, looked at Victorio's blank face, then returned his gaze to the floor.

"I would like to discuss an arrangement."

"What arrangement, Señor?"

The silence in the room was beginning to make Gabriel extremely uncomfortable.

"I would settle money on her, of course. A large sum. In her name."

"How much, Señor?"

"It would be an amount we agree upon, Victorio."

Gabriel began to relax. He liked Victorio. He had watched him grow up into an enterprising, ambitious young man. It was Victorio who had come to Gabriel when he needed money to help his mother begin the restaurant; and it was Victorio who had repaid the loan within two years. He had always seen Victorio as an excellent business risk. Even so, Gabriel knew his offer must be made with the formality of a marriage proposal. But he was not, of course, proposing marriage. Victorio understood this without needing an embarrassing explanation. They were two men who could find a solution for this situation.

"I need to speak to our mother. If she approves, then we will discuss the terms. If she does not approve, then I cannot help you, Gabriel. I hope you understand this."

"Yes. Yes, of course. You must discuss this with Señora Pérez. Explain to her, please, that I mean no disrespect. I would take care of Pilar, as if she were my lawful . . . wife. As if she were my wife, Victorio. Better than if she were my wife. Victorio, I would treat her better than I have ever treated my wife."

As Gabriel stumbled over himself in his declarations for Pilar, Victorio began to realize that this man just might be the key to their passage to California. He rose and offered his hand to Gabriel.

"I will speak to my mother. I will convince her as well as I can that this will be best for Pilar."

As Gabriel took Victorio's hand, he began to feel hope. He left the restaurant and walked through the village to his office above the store. He sat there late into the night, going over his personal accounts. It was the first time since his wedding day that he had not come home for dinner.

CHAPTER 7

"No!"

"Mamá, listen to me, please?"

"Listen to you? I should listen to you while you plan your sister's shame? How can you, Victorio?"

"I do not plan Pilar's shame, Mamá. I plan her happiness and her security. Her future. Please, think about it."

"I will not listen to you. How can you expect me to consider this for Pilar?"

"We must, Mamá. This is the one possibility for Pilar's future we never considered. There is no one for her to marry in this village."

"That does not mean I will agree to this plan. It is not right. Señor Calderón is not an honorable man."

"Yes he is, Mamá. Please listen to me? He will settle much money on Pilar. In her name, not in his. It will be her money, and I will see to it that it will be enough to ensure her security for the rest of her life. Think of what this will mean to her."

"Just exactly what do you propose this will mean to her, Victorio. Explain yourself to me!"

"Her freedom. Think of it. She will never want for anything, never be forced into a situation because of poverty. Mamá, we must not let her marry someone who will do nothing for her, where she will work herself to death with too many children and hardships. Do you want that for her? Do you, Mamá?"

Anger had helped Rosario keep her composure, but now the thought of Pilar living through what she had made her begin to cry.

"No, Victorio. I do not want this for Pilar."

"Then, consider this. Think about what Gabriel is offering. She will have a house, Mamá. I will see to it. A house in her name that no one can take from her."

"And what about her children, Victorio? Have you thought about that? They will have no name."

"It is my understanding this can be prevented. Jimena speaks of it all the time. Herbs. Remedies? Is this true?"

"Are you suggesting she have no children? How can you want that for Pilar? No children!"

"Mamá, she must not have children. You know this. This village is too small. Her children would be ridiculed. Gabriel's wife would see to that. It would be tragic if Pilar had children."

"You cannot be serious!"

"Of course, I am serious. You know I am right."

"I must be alone now, 'Torio. This is all so difficult. I have a lot to think about."

"I will leave you alone, but, understand, Mamá. This is the best we could ever do for Pilar. If you think carefully about it, you will realize that we could not do this well for her in a proper marriage. I will see to it that she has happiness from this. I promise you."

Victorio left the house and walked to the restaurant. Rosario remained seated in the parlor, stunned and unable to move. Juana entered from the kitchen and sat across the room from Rosario.

"Did you hear, Juana?"

"How could I help but hear such evil."

"Juana, you must help me decide. I cannot do this by myself."

"Why not? It is simple to decide. We cannot agree to this. We cannot place Pilar in such a situation. Señor Calderón is an old fool."

"But, Juana, he will take care of Pilar. She will not want for anything."

"Expect respectability. But, then, I guess that is not important to this family anymore. Certainly it is not important to Victorio!"

"It is important! Of course, it is! But, how can we offer that to her otherwise? There is no one here to offer respectability to Pilar. What will become of her, Juana? Do you ever think of this?"

"Yes, I think of it. That sweet child has no future here, I know that. For this reason, Rosario, we must protect her. You and I. She has no one else."

"But, we will not always be around to take care of her. Victorio has his family. So does Carlos. And we cannot count on Eduardo."

The noonday sun rose, burning yet another hot, dusty day onto the roofs of the village. Rosario and Juana remained in the parlor, discussing Pilar's future. Finally, Rosario left to work in the restaurant. Pilar had been helping Victorio with the accounts, but she returned to the house when Rosario arrived.

Victorio approached Rosario in the kitchen.

"Have you thought about Señor Calderón's offer?"

"Yes, Victorio, but I need more time. This is not something I will decide in one morning!"

"I understand, Mamá. I will tell Gabriel to wait."

October, 1945—Santa Barbara

In the fall of 1945, my Grandmother Isobel rejoiced at having her youngest sons home safely from the war in Europe. She had refused to cook her usual family dinners on Sundays until all her children could sit down together again. Her thirty-nine-year-old son, Rafael Velásquez, was soon to arrive from San Francisco, where he worked as a stockbroker. Then, and only then, would Isobel begin the Sunday celebration of reunion she had prayed for since the war began.

As she sat on her veranda waiting for the first of her sons and their wives to arrive, she examined the roses and chrysanthemums she held in her hand. The breeze ruffled the petals of the flowers as she contemplated the family's journey in 1918 from Spain to Hawaii and ultimately to California. She and her husband, Salvador, had left Spain with their small children to prevent twelve-year-old Rafael from being conscripted into the military. Her mother, being too old to travel across the ocean, had remained behind. She had sold the family property so she could give Isobel enough money for the family's survival in their new lives.

In 1924, when Rafael was eighteen, she had spent the remaining money to send him to San Francisco to finish his education. He had dutifully brought each of his brothers from Maui when they became of age. A successful businessman, Rafael had helped each brother get started in his own business, stood as best man at their weddings, and become godfather to his nieces and nephews. Now, Isobel lamented for her son. He should not be alone.

She heard the back door slam as someone entered the kitchen. Laughter echoed throughout the vast house as Isobel recognized the sound of her youngest child, her namesake, Isobel, whom everyone called Bella. She came bounding out to the veranda, pulling along her sixteen-year-old classmate and best friend, Teresita. Both of them were giggling, their cheeks flushed, their eyes bright.

"Mamá, this is Teresita. Isn't she pretty?"

Isobel looked at Teresita as she stood demurely before her. She was tiny, barely five feet tall. Her black hair was french-braided about her small, neat head. She was dressed in a white lawn dress, the bodice intricately pleated. Bella stood next to her, pleased with her friend.

"How do you do, Teresita. I am happy to meet you."

"I am happy to meet you also, Señora. Thank you for inviting me to your home today."

Isobel liked Teresita immediately. She could now understand why Bella had not spoken of anything or anyone else for weeks.

"Bella, come into the house with me. You and Teresita can set the table. Soon, everyone will arrive. I must finish the soup."

Teresita watched as Bella lifted down a flat, wooden chest from one of the cupboards in the dining room. She looked about her and was nearly blinded by the reflection of sunlight coming through the small leaded windows onto the white linen tablecloth. She had never seen such a long dining table. Silently, she helped Bella take the heavy silverware from the chest and set it about the table for fourteen people. Bella carefully handed the china to Teresita. Crystal water goblets followed, and then wine glasses. Finally, Bella set the heavy silver candleholders at each end of the table.

"There, that should just about do it. Let's go to my room before Mamá gives us more work to do. Come on."

The girls left the dining room and entered Isobel's bedroom. It was necessary to pass through her room to reach Bella's. Teresita paused at the threshold of Isobel's room. Everything in it was white. A white-crocheted duvet cover was on a white-painted bed. The headboard nearly reached the ceiling and was trimmed in delicate gold leaf. On the bed were three dolls. Teresita had never seen dolls like this. They looked like grown ladies. Their gowns were crocheted in mauve, violet, and rose. Their eyes stared at Teresita as she followed Bella past the crocheted lace curtains and into Bella's room. Here, everything was white and pink, again the crocheted lace was everywhere. Teresita was speechless. She watched as Bella stood in front of a beveled mirror and began brushing her short hair. Frustrated with the tangles, she threw the brush back onto the bureau.

"Come on, I'll show you the rest of the house."

Teresita dumbly followed. As they reached the front of the house, they heard a commotion from the living room.

"It's my brothers and sisters. They've arrived."

Bella began running through the house toward the living room, but Teresita, completely intimidated now, held back. She sat in a brocaded chair in the dining room, nervously smoothing her skirt. Almost immediately, the family entered the room. As they began taking their seats, all noisily talking at once, Bella led Teresita to a chair. She tried to make herself as small as possible, hoping no one would notice her. She stared at the china plate before her and did not see

Rafael sitting on the other end of the table, quietly studying her.

Isobel entered the room, holding high in front of her an immense soup tureen. She placed it in front of Teresita and lifted the lid with a flourish. A wonderful aroma of chicken soup wafted its way toward Teresita's face, helping her to relax. She smiled up at Isobel and then looked into the soup tureen. Bobbing stupidly in the center of the tureen was the head of the chicken, its eyes staring directly at Teresita. She gasped and fainted, falling to the side toward Bella. Her friend desperately propped her up as best she could, while Isobel stood in shock. Everyone at the table became completely silent as Rafael rushed to Teresita and carried her into the living room. Bella ran after Rafael. She felt terrible for not warning her friend about the Spanish tradition of floating the chicken's head in the soup and presenting it to a guest. Isobel looked dolefully at her youngest son, Salvador, Jr. Not yet graduated from high school, he had his head down on the table. He was laughing silently and uncontrollably. He caught sight of his mother and quickly left the table. Isobel could hear him continue his laughter, unchecked now, in the backyard.

My father, Rafael, followed the eight-hundred-year tradition of his family and visited my Grandmother Rosario the next day while Teresita was at school. Between them, they arranged the marriage that took place two years later between him and Teresita. During those two years, my father came from San Francisco to Santa Barbara every weekend to visit my mother. They would take drives in the country in my father's new car, my Grandmother Rosario sitting in the back seat. He would take both of them to the Mexican dances every Saturday night, my grandmother sitting along the walls with the other mothers, never taking her eyes off them.

Now, as I look back on this story of my parents' meeting, their courtship, their marriage, I have to wonder. As Rosario sat there at the dances watching her daughter, did she think of her own rebellion nearly forty years earlier? Did she realize that in the marriage she had arranged for her youngest daughter she was giving in to all she had defied? Or, was she remembering her dance with Alejandro, away from Juana's watchful eyes, the night they met? Rosario at thirteen dancing in the arms of Alejandro, an indio who would be unacceptable to her father. I believe my grandmother knew what she was doing with my mother's life. After the hardships she had suffered all her life to ensure the survival of her children, and realizing the tragic mistake of Pilar's arrangement, Rosario was now seeing to Teresita's survival by returning to the traditions she had rejected.

CHAPTER 8

Gabriel Calderón was undaunted by Victorio's request for time to consider his proposal. In love for the first and only time in his life, he began to neglect his businesses. He rode every morning, covering the vast acreage of his estate. Two properties had been joined together upon his marriage to Hermelina since both of them were the only heirs to their fathers' properties. The ranch would be divided only upon their deaths, when Christino and Eugenio would share it. But for now, Gabriel could still enjoy owning such a fine and beautiful property. He rode for hours every day, sometimes working his stallion into a lather. Then, he would dismount and walk the horse until it cooled. There were watering holes at close intervals, and often Gabriel would stop at one to share the lunch of one of his campesinos. There were many, for Gabriel would not dislodge them from the small plots of ground their families had farmed for generations. He believed he would invite the Fates to look disfavorably upon him if he caused another person unhappiness. He had always been fortunate, and attributed this to his attempts to be fair to everyone he encountered.

During his daily rides, he thought about Pilar. He had finally begun to catch brief glimpses of her in the village, but he had not attempted to speak to her. He did not want to frighten her. Already, he felt protective.

He found her a house on the outskirts of the village. He liked that. She would be shielded from the prying eyes of the villagers, at least somewhat. Certainly, it was better than if she lived in the village proper. He had quietly bought the house, but as yet had not furnished it. He would leave that to Pilar. It was her house now.

Gabriel would not entertain the possibility of Rosario's refusal. He could not imagine what he would do if his offer were rejected. Being a superstitious man, he believed that if he assumed success, he would have success.

Finally, after several weeks, Victorio summoned him. When Gabriel arrived at the restaurant, the sun was already setting. It was Sunday, so the restaurant was closed. Rosario was seated at one of the tables in the dining room. Victorio led Gabriel to the chair opposite Rosario. She was dressed in the formal clothes she wore to church. Her mother's pearls were about her neck.

"Señora Pérez. Thank you for consenting to meet with me. Before we begin, please let me say that I have the utmost respect for you, and for your family, and that whatever results from our conversation tonight, I will continue to hold you and your family in the highest esteem and consider you to be my friends."

"Thank you, Señor Calderón."

Victorio pulled out the remaining chair at the table and sat down. No one said anything else, so he began.

"Gabriel, my mother and I have discussed your offer and we have given it much consideration. We want what is best for Pilar, what will make her happiest."

Gabriel could not breathe. Were they going to say no? He thought he felt a slight pain in his chest, but disregarded it, for he could not take his eyes off Rosario. Try as he might, he could not read the decision on her face. He turned to Victorio but failed to determine anything there, either.

"Yes, of course. Pilar's happiness is the most important thing to consider here. I have many plans to ensure that happiness. I would welcome any suggestions from you, Señora, and from you, Victorio."

"I have told my mother of the security you intend to establish for Pilar. My mother has also requested that a house be purchased and placed in Pilar's name."

Gabriel began to breathe more easily; he thought of the house he had bought for Pilar.

"That will be done! Is there anything else? I want to demonstrate to you, Señora, that Pilar's happiness will always come first for me, before anyone else's."

Gabriel could no longer contain his joy. He began smiling as he took Rosario's hands into his.

"She will have whatever she desires. I am a wealthy man and all of my personal assets will be at her disposal. She will never want for anything."

Rosario gently pulled her hands out of Gabriel's. She stood up and moved away from the table.

"You must understand, Señor Calderón, I agree to this only out of concern for my daughter's happiness. I trust that you will never do anything to dishonor her."

"No, no. Never. Please understand, I have the highest regard for Pilar. Señora Pérez, I love your daughter. I will never bring harm to her."

"Nor will you allow anyone else to harm her, Señor?"

"Who would want to hurt Pilar?"

"Your sons, Señor Calderón. Eugenio and Christino. And your wife. What of your wife?"

"She will be protected from my family, Rosario. I promise you."

Rosario looked at Victorio. He was staring at the table in front of him. She carefully returned her attention to Gabriel, who was now standing next to Victorio. The silence in the room grew heavier as he and Victorio waited for Rosario's final word.

"Victorio, tomorrow you will accompany Señor Calderón to the bank and see to your sister's security."

She looked at Gabriel sternly.

"Pilar is very young, Señor. She will live a long life. I will hold you responsible for her well-being to the end of her days. Tomorrow, you and Victorio will search for a house. When the papers showing the house to be in her name are in my hands, I will tell Pilar."

"Señora, what if Pilar does not agree to our arrangement?"

Rosario stared at Gabriel for a long moment.

"She will agree, Señor."

After Rosario left the restaurant, Gabriel sat at the table opposite Victorio and held out his hand.

"Thank you, my friend. You have done me an honor tonight. I can never repay you."

Taking Gabriel's hands in his, Victorio did not reply. The last of the daylight had disappeared through the windows. Victorio rose and went into the kitchen. He returned with a bottle of tequila and some limes. Taking two small glasses from the shelves in the dining room, he sat at the table with Gabriel. He poured the tequila to the rims of the glasses and carefully pushed one in front of Gabriel.

"My respects, Gabriel."

"To Pilar, Victorio. To her happiness."

Together they drank the contents in one quick gulp. Squeezing the limes into their mouths, they proceeded to take turns filling each other's glasses again, and again.

Jimena found them asleep the next morning, their heads together on the table, the tequila bottle empty. Standing above them, their glasses in her hands, she surveyed the scene.

"Borrachos!"

Jimena went into the kitchen and deliberately began banging pans together.

The silent war regarding my arranged marriage continued between my parents, but I was often unaware of it. I was too busy playing with my brothers and the other seven boys in the neighborhood. I didn't play with girls. They were sissies. They played with dolls and plastic dishes; I carried a Boy Scout knife, a flashlight, and a length of rope for climbing trees. When I was thirteen, I took a dare and rode my bicycle down the steepest hill in the neighborhood.

It was a choking hot, Indian summer's day. Even the frogs by the creek were silent. At the bottom of the hill there was a deep ditch filled with dried blackberry bushes, their spikes like stilettos, tough and deadly. They were waiting for me that day, but none of us knew it.

We gathered at the top, our bikes crowding each other for space and a view. The object of the dare was to coast the bicycle down, hold on tightly as it gathered speed, gain enough speed to leap the ditch, then finesse the bicycle away from the massive oak tree that grew at the bottom. One of the boys, Bobby Russell, said I couldn't do it. His challenge was all I needed.

I had a brand-new blue bicycle from the previous Christmas. It had sparkled, brilliant in the glowing lights of the Christmas tree. I had begged for it for months. I stripped it of its fussy basket and dismantled the metal seat that ran the length of the back fender. No one was riding on the back of this bike. It would slow me down. To make certain no one *tried to ride on the fender, I removed it too. Finally, I was ready for action.*

The hill was so tall and steep, we could not see the bottom of the path, nor could we see the ditch, but we knew it was there. I gave myself an extra push with my sneakered foot, and began my descent into hell. Bumps and potholes jarred my teeth; I bit my tongue. What had I gotten myself into? The bicycle was an entity unto itself, for as it rapidly gathered speed, I lost control of it. When the bicycle hit the far edge of the ditch, we parted company. The oak tree lovingly embraced its sparkling blue frame as the bicycle wrapped its state-of-the-art, pumped-up tires around the trunk. I was thrown backward into the ditch and the waiting, voracious blackberry bushes.

The rest is hearsay.

Mr. Rider, the principal of our elementary school, lived at the top of the hill. I remember his house had a neat red tile roof and a flagstone patio in the back of his house. I saw it for the first time when I awoke lying on it.

The children ran down to the ditch to survey the wreckage and found me in the bushes, covered with blood. I wore only a pair of shorts and a halter, and there was no part of me that was not gouged and torn by the brambles. They ran crying to Mr. Rider and he carried me up the hill to his patio. My youngest brother raced his bicycle home to tell my mother that I was dead. She believed him, of course.

She arrived at Mr. Rider's house as I was emerging from unconsciousness. My father came from his office to take me to the doctor. I was wrapped in a blanket and carried to the car past the now-subdued crowd of children craning their necks to catch another glimpse of the victim. My eyes met with Bobby's.

He knew.

That night I overheard my parents talking in the living room. I was in bed bandaged like a mummy and aching all over. They were discussing my face and possible plastic surgery. My father assured my mother of what the doctor had said: As I grew up, the scars would disappear.

Later, my father came into my room and sat on the bed. Surveying the damage, he said, "Amparo, you know I love you, don't you?"

"Yes, Daddy."

I waited for the rest. I knew what was coming. I needed desperately to know when I could have a new bike. How could I live without one?

"Your mother loves you very much, too. You understand this, don't you?"

"Yes, Daddy."

"Amparo, I will never buy you another bicycle. Please, sweetheart, don't ever ask me for one."

I was in bed for a week, but finally I was allowed to rejoin the neighborhood children. The first project I had in mind was to acquaint Bobby Russell with his Waterloo. I found him and kept the promise that passed between us as my father carried me to his car a week earlier. I bloodied Bobby's nose, then I banged his head on the cement driveway of his house. He never again told me I couldn't do something because I was a girl.

CHAPTER 9

1928—Hermosillo

Rosario and Juana accompanied Pilar to her new home. No one in the village was yet aware of the arrangement, so no one took notice as the three women laden with linens and Pilar's clothing walked to the house. The house was not furnished, but Gabriel had left catalogs so Pilar could choose what she wanted for her home.

They entered a tiled hall that opened onto the stairs leading to the upper floor. The hall was dark and cool, welcoming them after their long walk. Pilar placed her parcels on the floor and ran upstairs. She was eager and excited to explore the house. She didn't understand why Señor Calderón would buy it for her, but Victorio and her mother had convinced her it was because he cared about her and her welfare. She had seen Señor Calderón only twice, each time when she had gone to his store. Once, he had been in the back room speaking to one of the customers, the other time, two weeks ago, he had added up her purchases.

In her new home there was a hallway at the top of the stairs. It ran the full length of the house and turned the corners, forming a carved, wooden balcony around the center of the upper floor. A red-tiled roof overhung the balcony, protecting Pilar from the hot sunlight as she looked down on the courtyard at the center of the house. She ran back to the top of the stairs.

"Mamá, Juana! Come! Hurry!"

Frightened by Pilar's outburst, they rushed up the stairs to find Pilar bending over the banister, her cheeks flushed with excitement, her eyes dancing with joy.

"Look, there is a courtyard. Look at it, Mamá. A fountain and a little pool."

Pilar turned and raced down the stairs, then through the hallway to the French doors that opened onto the courtyard. She stopped in the middle of the flagstones, her eyes wide with excitement. She turned to the left and right, trying to see every corner and detail.

Rosario and Juana could not keep pace with her. She ran back through the house, pausing in the dining room, in the parlor, only to rush out again and back upstairs. There were four large rooms on either side of the banistered hallways, with each balcony window shuttered for privacy. One room, the largest, had its own bath and adjoining sitting room. It was here that Juana and Rosario caught up with Pilar. She was sitting in the center of the room, a look of delight and happiness on her face.

"Oh, Mamá. Isn't it a beautiful house? Isn't it wonderful?"

Juana inspected the bath and sitting rooms, and then rejoined Pilar and Rosario in the bedroom. The wall opposite the balcony was paneled in stained glass, with red and purple flowers gracing the leaded panes. The light threw itself in muted colors upon the floor and walls. It was a beautiful room.

"I will be very happy in this house. You were right, Mamá. This is the best thing for me to do."

She rose and went to Juana. "Let's go find the kitchen."

They left the room together as Rosario continued to explore the upper floor. She found a large room with many built-in shelves. Someone once had a library here, she thought. Will Pilar have books? She will need something to occupy her days and nights. Rosario knew Pilar could be spending time alone in this house. Would she be happy? Had Rosario done the right thing for her daughter? Sighing, she left the room and went downstairs to join Pilar and Juana.

"Look, this will be your room, Juana. Will you like it? It has more light and is larger than your room at home."

Juana looked at Pilar, saw her happiness and began to relax. Her decision to live with Pilar had encountered little resistance from the rest of the family. They needed her help with the grandchildren, but they also realized that Pilar must not again feel abandoned by them.

"This room will be fine, little one. I will be very happy here."

The dining room was across the hall from the kitchen. Small and intimate, it was nestled beneath the staircase. The window in this room was also of stained glass. A peacock, prismatic and elegant, reflected its jewel-like colors onto Pilar's hair and dress.

After surveying the rest of the house they returned to Rosario's, taking the catalogs with them. Within a few days Pilar, with their help, had chosen the furnishings for the entire house. Victorio took the list to Gabriel, who proceeded to place the orders, never questioning Pilar's choices.

Gabriel notified Victorio of each delivery during the ensuing weeks. Pilar and Juana would hurry to the house, unlock the doors for the deliveries, and spend the rest of the day placing and replacing the furniture until Pilar was satisfied with the arrangement. Finally the house was furnished and she and Juana moved in.

CHAPTER 10

Gabriel waited a week before he visited Pilar. When he arrived, Juana escorted him into the parlor. He carried a small box and as he entered the room, he presented it to Pilar, who was sitting on a pale blue, brocaded chair and dressed in a soft pink silk gown she had embroidered with small yellow flowers.

She accepted the box silently and watched as Gabriel sat on the sofa across from her. Neither spoke. Pilar lifted the lid of the box and found inside a string of creamy white pearls. She took them out of the satin-lined interior. They reflected the pale pink of her dress and glowed in her hands as if they were alive.

Raising her eyes to Gabriel, she was speechless.

"Those are Majorca pearls, Pilar. I ordered them especially for you. I wanted to give you something beautiful on our first visit."

"Thank you, Señor Calderón."

"Please, Pilar, will you call me Gabriel?"

Pilar looked at him, unable to understand. She could not imagine calling him by his first name. It would be disrespectful, so she said nothing.

Gabriel waited for her to reply, then clumsily continued.

"Do you like your house, Pilar? If you don't, I will buy you another. I want you to be happy."

"I like this house, Señor."

She spoke barely above a whisper, and after her first examining look kept her gaze on the floor, her head down. Gabriel watched her intently, taken by her beauty. Her hair was in a braid intertwined with a golden ribbon and coiled high on the back of her head like a crown. Soft tendrils curled upon the nape of her neck.

"Is there anything you need? For yourself, the house? You only have to tell me, Pilar. You will have whatever you need."

She raised her eyes to Gabriel's once again, but did not reply. Gabriel returned her gaze and thought of broken crystals reflecting upon an aquamarine sea. He remembered a sea like this when he was a small boy. He and his parents had sailed from Spain to Mexico when he was seven and he had spent the endless days holding to the railing and staring at the ocean waves lapping at the ship's wooden hull. He had not thought of this for years.

Suddenly self-conscious, he looked around the room and noticed how tastefully Pilar had furnished it. Everything was delicate and in pastel colors. His house was furnished with heavy oak, browns, burgandies, blacks, somberness. Here, he felt as if he had shed his worries and responsibilities at the front door.

"I am glad you are happy here."

Pilar looked down at her hands holding the pearls and then back at Gabriel.

"Thank you for the pearls, Señor. They are lovely." Gabriel reluctantly rose, walked across the room, and stood in front of Pilar.

"May I come to see you again tomorrow, Pilar?"

"Yes, Señor."

After he left, Pilar remained on her chair holding the pearls. She reached for the box and carefully replaced them on their satin pillow. She held the box on her lap for a long time before noticing the sun was nearly down. It had turned the room a deep mauve, casting its shadows upon her dress and hands. Placing the velvet box on the table next to her, she rose and went in search of Juana.

My fourteenth birthday had arrived, and still I had not been sent to Spain. We were all painfully aware of my parents' alienation, but I didn't understand it. I only knew there was periodic tension, a stillness as if the house held its breath: The atmosphere wrapped itself around me, established my rhythms, choked me.

The taut wire that held my parents together snapped one night after dinner when my mother and I were washing the dishes. I knew she was upset; I could feel her tension growing in the way she moved about the kitchen. Suddenly, she took a piece of china to the kitchen door that led downstairs and threw it into the family room. She turned and took every piece of china, one at a time, from the dish drainer and threw it after the first. The cupboard's contents followed. One dish after the other smashed against the family room wall. My father and brothers were in the living room and, of course, heard the commotion, but nobody moved. When there were no dishes left, my mother walked into the living room and stood in front of my father.

"Amparo will marry whom she pleases!"

No one spoke. My mother went into their bedroom and slammed the door. My father looked at me, a stunned expression on his face. I went to my bedroom and sat on my bed. I finally knew the answer to my puzzlement of so many years. Lines had been drawn—with my father and Grandmother Isobel on one side, demanding that I be sent

to Spain, the contract kept; my mother on the other side, refusing to comply.

The tension changed after that night. My mother never
let down her defenses, fearful if her guard dropped for a moment my grandmother and father would spirit me away. So
a détente was established between my parents, but my grandmother never joined into this negotiated peace. She remained
aloof and condemning, predicting disaster for me if I were allowed to marry just anybody. To reinforce her disapproval,
she refused to attend my wedding five years later in 1969.

Dressed in my wedding gown, I was taken to my grandmother's house before proceeding to the church. I knelt before
her, my gown billowing about me in clouds of white or-
ganza. A crown of seed pearls held a seven-layered veil of
tulle netting. I was an empty vessel, nervous and frightened.
Lightheaded, I listened to my grandmother give me my
blessing. Then, she said to me,

"Amparo, you are the end result of eight-hundred years
of carefully arranged marriages, hand-chosen bloodlines. Today, you will break faith with your ancestors, deny your responsibilities to your children, and end a tradition carefully
guarded by generations of Velásquez. I cannot witness this
destruction. Never forget who you are! Never forget where
you come from!"

CHAPTER 11

Pilar filled her days attending to the house. The kitchen and heavier cleaning were Juana's domain, but Pilar spent many hours fussing with and rearranging furniture, changing the curtains at the windows, dusting, polishing. In exasperation, Juana took her aside. Sitting her in the parlor, she spoke to Pilar.

"One day, Pilar, the Devil realized he was lonely. So, he decided to create for himself a child, to keep him company. He wanted this child to be perfect so he began to fuss with him. He fixed his arm just so, his leg just so. He fixed his hair, remolded his ears, added more teeth. He decided to adjust his child's smile so it would be more joyous, until suddenly, he poked it in the eye!" Letting go of Pilar's arm Juana waited for a reply. Pilar looked at Juana, an ingenuous expression on her face, then she fell over onto the couch in uncontrollable laughter.

"Oh, Juana, that is a delightful story. Where did you hear it?"

"From my grandmother," she answered somberly. "You must let it be a warning to you."

Giggling now, Pilar replied, "Yes, Juana."

She rose and ran from the room, her laughter bubbling behind her, leaving Juana to mutter her way back to the kitchen.

Gabriel continued to come daily. They would visit

in the parlor, Gabriel stumbling over himself trying to make conversation with Pilar. She, self-conscious and flattered by his attention, would remain silent. Gabriel never lost patience with her, rather he was charmed by her innocence. He wanted to be closer to her but didn't know how to achieve this.

"I know I ask you this every time I come here, but is there anything you need, something perhaps that I have forgotten?"

Pilar was dressed in a white, three-tiered sundress she had embroidered with colorful parrots. Gabriel was uplifted by the gaiety of her dress. Before he realized what she was doing, Pilar went to him and began to reach for his hand. Catching herself, she pulled her hand away.

"Excuse me, Señor."

"Is there something, Pilar?"

"Yes, there is."

Taking her hand in his, he noticed she did not pull away.

Encouraged, Gabriel said, "Show me, Pilar."

She led him through the house and out into the courtyard. They stood in the center of the flagstones, Pilar still holding his hand.

"Flowers, Gabriel," she whispered. "I would like flowers, over here and here, and over there."

Pulling him along, she began to circle the edges of the patio, pointing out the areas where she wanted blooms and color.

"Here, I would like liana, and over there, more climbing vines. Jasmine here to wind its way up to the balcony. I would train it. It would smell so sweet."

"I will send gardeners tomorrow."

"No! I do not want gardeners to do this. I will do it. Please, Gabriel. No gardeners!"

Seeing her distress, he quickly calmed her.

"Of course, you may do this yourself."

Circling the courtyard thoughtfully, he added, "Would you let me help you?"

He looked at her hopefully. "I was once a very good gardener. I would enjoy helping you."

"Yes, Gabriel. I would like that."

Her eyes were shining with gratitude. She could not take them off Gabriel. Slowly, he walked toward her. Taking her face between his hands, he kissed her softly on the forehead.

"Your happiness is more important to me, Pilar, than my own. You know this, don't you?"

"I am beginning to understand. Yes, I think I understand."

"Good! Tomorrow we will start. I will bring the lianas. I will find the jasmine. I will be back in the morning, early, with the sunrise. We will have this garden for you."

She was overwhelmed with delight. For weeks Gabriel had brought her gifts of jewelry, beautiful fabrics, even candy from Mexico City. She had accepted each gift with a formality that left Gabriel frustrated and lonely. Finally, he had found the gift that brought profound happiness to her eyes. How simple were her wants and needs. When he left the house he walked with a buoyancy he thought he had lost as a young man.

Pilar ran through the house looking for Juana.

When she found her, she began dancing the old woman around the dining room.

"Flowers, Juana. I am to have flowers. Any flowers I want."

"What are you talking about?"

"The courtyard. Gabriel and I are going to plant flowers and vines in the courtyard. Starting tomorrow!"

Pilar let go of Juana and ran upstairs. Hanging over the banister, she watched Juana follow her from the dining room.

"Roses, Juana. Pink roses. Red ones. We will have a jungle of roses."

Disappearing up the stairs, Pilar did not hear Juana mumble as she made her way to the kitchen.

"Roses! Jasmine! Gabriel! What is this? I am surrounded by foolish old men and foolish children."

I was nineteen when I first met Peter. I had been married seven months, and my husband and I had moved to San Francisco so he could go to school. He worked part-time in a bank in the Marina. Peter banked there and befriended my husband. He invited us to dinner, and I met him that evening.

He had a devastating impact on my nineteen-year-old mind. I didn't know what to make of him. He was ebullient and so dynamic I realized I was forgetting to breathe as I watched him talk to my husband. Silently, I studied him. He appeared to be paying me little regard, except for solicitous attentions, such as pulling out my chair for me, admiring my dress. He was forty-two, polished, at ease in the expensive restaurant. He ordered wine and joked with the waiter. He knew him by name, knew the names of his children, asked after them. I was running mentally to keep up with him. Too young for Peter, not so much in years but in my ability to withstand my emotions, I gave up to his presence, his onslaught. I left my husband within the first year of our marriage and went to live with Peter in defiance of all I had been taught by my family's traditions.

Peter owned a plantation in El Salvador. The first year, we went to Central America. I didn't like it there. It was hot, humid; my skin couldn't breathe. I wanted to return to San Francisco, to cool ocean breezes. I missed the haunting sounds of foghorns and the waves on the rocks beneath our house, but the harvest was to begin. The campesinos would not start until Peter, the patrón, rode his horse through the plantation. The first time, I rode with him, but I felt strange, out of place. Behind him, my horse was skittish; the campesinos stared at me silently. I knew Peter hated his role, but he explained he could not go against tradition, that it would be a sign of disrespect.

For five years, we continued going to El Salvador. We would leave in November, the beginning of the harvest season, and fly to the village of La Libertad. We would return to San Francisco in April and live there in our home by the ocean until the following November. In 1976, so many of the people in El Salvador carried guns, even the children. On Peter's instructions, I stayed in the house while he began the harvest. For the first time, he wore a gun and holster, and left John, his pilot, with me. I noticed that both of them never went out unarmed.

CHAPTER 12

"I don't think that rose bush should be planted there."

"Why not?" Gabriel held the roots of the rose bush in his gloved hand above the hole he had just dug for it.

"It will grow very large in the sunlight, then it will bump its head on that overhang above it."

"Bump its head? Roses do not have heads, Pilar."

"Yes, they do. Don't plant it there!"

Gabriel looked at her. She was kneeling over a flowerbed he had prepared the previous day. Her hands were black with dirt. No matter how hard he tried to convince her to wear gloves, she refused.

"You have to feel the dirt, Gabriel. Touch it. Smell it. Become a part of it. It will not grow flowers for you if you do not become a part of it."

She had dirt on her face. The front of her dress was covered with it; Juana would have to throw the dress away. But her expression was everything Gabriel had dreamed of since the day he first saw her.

"Where do you want this rose bush, Pilar?"

She sat back onto the flagstones and surveyed the courtyard. Every niche was filled with blooms. Vines were already beginning to wend their way up to the balcony. The jasmine was in place and Pilar checked it every day for blossoms, even though Gabriel had told her it would be months before they would begin to shower their petals about the courtyard.

"Let's put it over there beneath that wall. It will get enough sun, but not bump its head on anything."

Humoring her, he took the rose bush across the patio and began to dig a hole for it. Juana entered the courtyard with a large tray carrying their lunch. She had brought the tray every day, laden with food. Gabriel and Pilar sat at the large wooden table they had placed to the left of the French doors and feasted on Juana's largesse.

"So. Yesterday, you were telling me about Sister Carmelina. About her attempts to teach you French."

Pilar began to laugh.

"Oh, Gabriel. She was so funny. I tried to make my mouth form the vowels, but after a day of speaking with her, my mouth would hurt. I told her human beings are not meant to speak French. She would get so angry with me."

"And did you finally learn the language?"

She had washed her hands and her face before sitting down to lunch, but had missed a spot on her forehead. Gabriel reached out to wipe it with his hand. Pilar shied away. She didn't notice she had pulled away from him, but instead kept on talking about her experience in the convent. Gabriel was puzzled. Sometimes he was able to put his arms around her, but often when he attempted to touch her face, Pilar would maneuver herself away from him. It was done so skillfully that Gabriel was often unsure if she had evaded his touch, or if he had simply missed. He studied her as she continued talking.

"Sometimes, we would play tricks on Sister Carmelina."

"Who?"

"Sister Carmelina. I just told you."

"No. Who would play the tricks with you?"

"Francesca. She was a novice. She was my friend."

"How old were you then?"

"Fifteen."

"What happened to Francesca?"

"She will take her vows next year."

"Did you ever want to be a nun, Pilar?"

Pilar looked around the courtyard, then up toward the sky.

"No. Francesca wanted me to stay. We were the same age, and we were very lonely. I didn't want to leave her, but I didn't want to be a nun."

"Why not?"

He poured her some more wine.

"Well, you see, Gabriel, there is so much they can-not do."

"Give me an example."

"They cannot speak. All day, they do not speak. Until Francesca arrived when I was fourteen, I had no one to talk to, except the Mother Superior."

"There were no other children at the convent?"

"No. I don't know why. I always hoped for more, but they never came."

Gabriel continued watching her. She had finished her glass of wine and her cheeks were reddening. The sunlight fell on her hair, causing the braids to glisten; tendrils escaped about her face, damp and curling. Sometimes Gabriel felt he was in a trance when he watched her. She was devoid of self-consciousness, not at all as she had been when she first came here. She had grown comfortable with him. When he arrived, she was happy and excited to see him. He came every day now, staying longer, leaving later, oblivious to his family's complaints. He was obsessed and happier than he had ever been.

"So, you were alone much of the time. What did you do?"

"I had a courtyard like this. Oh, it wasn't so fine. There were mostly roses. And there were lemons."

Pilar rose from her chair and, suddenly nervous, walked over to the wall next to them. Her back to Gabriel, she seemed to leave him, float away into her thoughts.

"Lemons?"

"Yes, I seem to remember. Lemons . . ."

"Pilar, you have not finished your lunch. Come back to the table. Let us finish, then we will continue planting the roses."

She turned to him, a puzzled look on her face. She was distressed, but she returned to her chair. Gabriel poured her another glass of wine, then added water to it. He was concerned with the flushed expression on her face.

CHAPTER 13

The branches of the jasmine were dark and shiny, turning gently in the soft breezes, as dusk's shadows dappled the courtyard. Juana entered the green haven and was instantly enchanted by it. No longer bare, it was filled with lush vegetation. Gabriel and Pilar had worked for two weeks, Gabriel arriving early every morning to find Pilar already up and eagerly waiting for him.

Walking through the courtyard, Juana inspected their work. There were orchids, violets, gardenias. Where did Gabriel get them? Continuing along the mossy edges of the flagstones, she circled to the right, past ferns, lianas and star jasmine. There, nestled among miniature orange trees just beginning to bloom with waxy white blossoms, she discovered Gabriel and Pilar lying together on the large chaise under the balcony. They had fallen into an exhausted sleep, Gabriel on his back, snoring lightly, Pilar alongside him, her head nestled in his arms. The ribbons Juana had woven into the braids that morning were scattered about. Her hair rippled over Gabriel's arm and flowed onto the flagstones.

Juana backed away, continuing to look at them as the shadows gradually darkened the entire courtyard. She turned and silently made her way into the house. In her room she packed a few belongings. She was an intruder now. Juana had come to trust Gabriel during the past weeks and now Pilar was happy with him and her home. Juana let herself out the front door as quietly as possible. She noticed the wind was rising. There was the smell of rain in the air as she walked across town in the dark to Rosario's.

CHAPTER 14

The wind awakened Pilar. She sat up in her bed and looked about. The odor of lemons filled her nostrils. In her dream, she had been running through the lemon grove, the wind knocking her to the ground, the dirt grinding under her fingernails when she tried to get up.

She turned and looked down at Gabriel. He was in a deep sleep, his arm across her stomach. Carefully, feeling dazed, she rose from the bed and crossed the room to the window. One shutter was banging against the window frame, the other had broken off and fallen to the balcony. The wind, a near gale now, was rhythmically lifting the shutter and letting it clatter back to the ground. Pilar stared at it a moment, then opened the balcony door.

Pushing against the force of the gale, she walked to the shutter and lifted it. The wind took it from her hand and tossed it below to the courtyard. Looking at the sky, searching through the clouds for the moon, Pilar held onto the handrail until she reached the top of the stairs. Following the scent of the lemons in her dream, she started down the stairs. Halfway there she began to cry. Clinging to the railing, she lowered herself until she was sitting on a step. Her memories overwhelmed her.

She was running from someone. Who was it? Her

body convulsed with sobs. Going from step to step, gripping the railing, Pilar continued down. She moved from pillar to pillar around the courtyard, clinging to the lianas, her sobbing out of control. She was trying to reach the rose bush Gabriel had planted for her that afternoon.

Gabriel awoke with a start. He reached for Pilar and realizing she was not in the bed, called her name into the roar of the wind. He rose and walked to the balcony door. He could see Pilar as she knelt by the far wall of the garden. His senses alerted by the gale, he ran out onto the balcony.

"Pilar!" he shouted.

He ran downstairs, holding to the railing and slipping several times on the stairs. It was raining now, large drops coming down in torrents. He could barely see Pilar through the curtains of rain that filled the courtyard.

"Pilar!"

Crossing to her he could see she was digging into the ground next to the rose bush. He tried to lift her from the ground, but she pulled away. Her nightgown was soaked; the delicate fabric had caught on the thorns of the rosebush. Her arms were bleeding where the barbs had torn her skin. Oblivious to her wounds, she continued digging. He reached under her, and though the wet gown made it difficult to get a secure grip, he lifted her from the ground.

"No! Let me go! Let me go!" she screamed, hitting him.

Struggling with her, he carried her up the stairs. By the time he reached the balcony, she had collapsed against him, sobbing uncontrollably and clinging to him. He carried her into the bedroom and placed her on the bed. From the adjoining bathroom he took one of the large towels and after removing her gown, wrapped Pilar in the towel. She huddled on the bed, crying quietly. Gabriel got another towel and dried himself, put on his clothes, and sat on the chair next to the bed. He watched Pilar.

"Sweetheart, tell me what is wrong? Did I do something to make you this unhappy? Tell me, please."

"No."

"No, I did not do something, or no, you will not tell me?"

"I cannot tell you, Gabriel."

"But, I thought you could tell me anything, and that I could you."

"Not this."

"Please, sit up, my darling. Look at me. Let me help you."

Pilar turned over and, struggling with a weariness even she did not understand, she slowly sat up and faced Gabriel. Her look of devastation overwhelmed him.

Apprehensive, he asked her, "Did I do this to you? Please forgive me. I would never hurt you. I love you more than my life."

"Gabriel, you did not do this. I'm not certain what is wrong with me. I feel so frightened."

"But I am here with you. I would never let anybody hurt you. You know this, don't you?"

He reached for her, but she left the bed. Wrapped

in the towel, Pilar went to the window. The rain, now lessened to a steady drizzle, was making a comforting sound on the flagstones. The wind had finally died down, too. The air was still and close.

"Something happened to me, Gabriel. In the convent. I hardly remember. Tonight, when I woke up, I remembered some of it."

"Can you tell me what you remember?"

Turning toward him, she was silhouetted against the window. He could not see her face, only the shape of her body wrapped in the towel, and her hair clinging to her shoulders.

"I think I was raped, Gabriel."

The sound of the rain filled Gabriel's ears. It was a few seconds before he realized it was his rage he heard. Doing his best to control himself, he asked her, "Tell me what happened to you. I want to know. I need to know if I am to help you."

"I played in the lemon grove outside the convent. I would sneak out while the nuns were taking their siesta."

"How old were you?"

"I was eleven."

Gabriel began to rise, then realized what he was doing and lowered himself back into the chair.

"Go on. What happened?"

"A man grabbed me. I tried to get away from him but he hit me many times."

She turned back to the window, her head down. She clung to the windowsill and watched the rain. Gabriel rose and went to her. Standing behind her, he did not touch her.

"Tell me the rest."

"I don't remember the rest, but I know now I was raped. I ran back to the convent and buried my dress by the rose bushes."

Her shoulders were hunched within the towel. Gabriel watched as they began to shake. A low keening escaped her, muffled against her shoulder. It rose higher and higher as Gabriel reached for her. He lifted and carried her to the rocking chair in the corner of the room. Sitting down, he began to rock her gently. He did not say anything to her, but instead he held her through the rest of the night.

Eventually, the sun poured its light into the room, bathing the man and the girl, both asleep. The girl was clinging to him as if he were the only barrier between her and the demons that chased her in dreams. The warmth of the sunlight caused the girl to stir, but the man only held her more tightly. As the morning progressed, the sunlight, finding the scene peaceful, passed on to other parts of the courtyard, leaving the room again in cool shadows. It settled itself upon the single rose bush nestled against the brick wall.

Gabriel did not leave Pilar alone until he was satisfied she was recovered. They rose at noon and together fixed breakfast. They carried it into the dining room and after Gabriel poured her chocolate, he began to peel a mango for Pilar. He carefully cut it into bite-size pieces and presented it to her.

"I love you, Gabriel."

"Of course you do, silly girl. We shall love each

other forever, but I shall not peel mangoes for you forever. Mustn't spoil you."

Giggling uncertainly, Pilar reached across the table and tried to feed Gabriel a roll.

"No. No. Only fruit in the morning for this old man."

"You are not old!"

"No, my darling. You have it wrong. You are not old!"

"We are not old, Gabriel. There. I have pronounced it. It is so!"

He looked at her for a long moment. Her eyes were slightly puffy and red-rimmed. She had brushed her hair, but not braided it. There was a glow about her, in spite of the ordeal she had just been through.

"Pilar, would you do something for me?"

"Yes, of course."

"Never come down to breakfast with your hair braided. Let me start my mornings like this for the rest of my life."

Looking down demurely at her hands in her lap, Pilar replied, "Yes, Señor."

"How come Aunt Pilar never had children?"

"She did."

I was puzzled. My mother and I were sitting in her living room. Aunt Pilar had just left. I had decided to come home to Santa Barbara for the holidays that winter, leaving Peter to his sailboat, his plantation, and the continuing unrest in Central America. It was 1977.

"What happened to her baby?"

"It died at birth."

"Was it a boy or a girl?"

"I don't know. No one has ever said. The family never talked much about it."

I studied my mother as I continued.

"What about your father? Who was he?"

"I never knew him. My brother Victorio told me he died when I was a baby."

"What did Uncle Victorio tell you about him? What was his name? Was it Pérez?"

"No. I don't know what his name was. Mamá separated from him before he died."

"Why did they give you the Pérez name and not his name?"

"Honey, I'm not certain. No one ever talked about it much. I think Mamá wanted to forget about him. I used to ask about this a lot when I was a little girl, but no one *would tell me the answers. I guess over the years I stopped wondering."*

"Momma, you don't look like Aunt Juanita, or Aunt María. You don't even look like Uncle Victorio. Your features are completely different. Haven't you ever wondered about that?"

"Well, sometimes the genes skip generations. You look just like your Aunt Pilar. Do you know that? It's probably why she spoils you so much."

CHAPTER 15

It had begun to rain again when Gabriel left Pilar's house. He was immensely troubled by what Pilar had told him the night before. She had always appeared fragile, but he thought it was because of her slenderness. Now, he realized the fragility came from within.

Needing to talk to someone, he stopped to see his old boyhood friend, Father Ruiz. They had grown up together, and while Gabriel was married and having his sons, Cleofas was learning to be a priest.

He returned to his village and after his ordination, he became the confessor to Gabriel's family, often dining with them on Sunday evenings after the late Mass.

Now, Cleofas sat in his chair behind the desk in the rectory and watched Gabriel.

"You look troubled, my friend."

"I am, I am, Cleofas."

"How is your family? Your wife?"

Gabriel looked up at the priest but did not answer.

The silence stretched between them. A chasm of years, triumphs celebrated, parents' deaths grieved over, all of this fell into the breach slowly opening between them.

"You know about Pilar."

"The entire town knows about Pilar. Have you

thought about what you are doing? To your wife, your children? To Pilar?"

Gabriel continued looking at the floor.

"Hermelina has been here to talk to me about this. What are you doing?"

"I am happy, Cleofas. For the first time in my life, I am happy!"

"But, at what expense! Do you know the cost to your family?"

"I have not abandoned my family!"

"No, I understand they want for nothing, except a father in their life, except, perhaps, respectability. Hermelina is at least entitled to that. If you insist on this sin, Gabriel, could you not be more discreet about it?"

"Cleofas, all of my life I have lived to please other people. My father, then my wife, then my children. I have worked hard to give them everything they need. I educated my sons. It was important to their mother. I agreed to her choices for wives for Eugenio and Christino. I have never denied her her wishes in anything. But, Cleofas, what about me? When am I entitled to something of my own, something that brings me happiness? Pilar is my joy now. She takes nothing from Hermelina."

"Except her husband and her pride."

"That is not Pilar's doing. It is mine."

"Gabriel, what you are doing is a sin. It is a sin against God's laws. You condemn yourself. You condemn Pilar."

"How can this much happiness be against any laws?"

"You know better. You are trying to justify what you do, but you know you are being selfish. You are causing pain to your family. You will cause pain to Pilar someday. What if she has a child?"

"Her mother and I have agreed she will not. We understand the impossibility of that."

"It has never been my understanding that you or Rosario have anything to say about God's plans, Gabriel! How can you be so arrogant?"

Gabriel had risen from his chair and was pacing the tiled floor of the rectory. Father Ruiz watched him.

"Go home to your wife, Gabriel. Give up this girl. It is a crime what you are doing."

"I cannot give her up!"

"If you don't, you will remove yourself from the blessings of the Sacraments. I will deny them to her also. Do you have the right to decide that for her?"

Gabriel stopped at the door, his hand on the knob.

"I must go to Hermelina and try to explain."

"She needs no explanation. She is prepared to forgive you and forget this escapade of yours. She knows it is her duty as your wife, and as the mother of your children. That is who she is, Gabriel, though you have forgotten this!"

"Good-bye, Cleofas."

After Gabriel had gone, Father Ruiz sat at his desk in silence. Tears began to form for his old friend. He wiped them away and left the office. In the chapel, he knelt in front of the Virgin, but he did not pray.

The rain was pounding into Gabriel. When he arrived at his house he was soaked to his skin. His man-servant, Julio, rushed to him and began peeling off his outerwear. Following Gabriel into his bedroom suite, he told him, "I will prepare a bath, Señor. You will become ill if you do not warm yourself. I will lay out your clothing while you are in the bath."

"No. Just get me dry things, Julio."

"But, Señor, you are shivering . . ."

"And, Julio, you are to pack my things, my clothes, my books, all my personal belongings. You are to take them to the small house on the edge of town."

Julio, his whole face aquiver with grief, answered his patrón. "Yes, Señor. With all respect, I know the house."

"Good. Do it now, Julio. Have the other servants help you. We will not be coming back after today."

Gabriel changed his clothes and went through the large hacienda looking for his wife. He found her in the solarium. Her two daughters-in-law were sitting beside her. Giving him harsh looks, they both rose and left the room when he entered.

"Gabriel. Can I get you anything? Some coffee? Something to eat? I will call the servants."

"No, Hermelina. I am not hungry."

He sat across the room from her.

"I have come from Cleofas."

She did not respond. Instead, she looked at him pleadingly. Her silence continued, making Gabriel more uncomfortable.

"I know that I have caused you distress."

She looked down at her lap and then back at Gabriel.

He said nothing for several moments.

"I have tried to be a good husband to you, the husband you have deserved, but I have failed you. I have failed our children. I never meant to bring you embarrassment."

"It has been difficult, but I forgive you, Gabriel. It is my duty to forgive you."

"Yes, I know. Cleofas told me."

He paused, and then continued.

"Perhaps, there has been too much done here out of duty, Hermelina. Our lives have been lived out of duty to each other. Hasn't that been difficult for you?"

She looked at him in bewilderment.

"I do not understand. Our life is duty. I have always known this. So have you, Gabriel."

"But, haven't you ever wanted anything else? Something for yourself?"

"No. I have everything I want right here. I have my sons, and my grandchildren. What else is there, Gabriel? Can you tell me?"

He looked around the room. It appeared barren and cold to him. The heavy, somber furniture was overwhelmingly depressing. He ached for Pilar's parlor, with its soft colors and sunlight. He ached for her presence. Returning his gaze to his wife, he answered her.

"I cannot tell you, Hermelina. I cannot tell you. I cannot stay here with you any longer, either. I am sorry. I know you cannot forgive me for this, but I am an old man here. I am dying here. I don't want to die."

She was appalled by his words. Her mouth opened,

but no sound came out. He rose from his chair and turned to leave the room.

"No, Gabriel!" she screamed. "You cannot leave us!"

He heard her screams as he walked through the house. He opened the front door and walked through it. Standing on the porch, he studied the rain. He could hear his sons' wives trying to comfort Herme- lina as he stepped off the porch. The rain pelted him with recrimination.

Slowly, Gabriel Calderón walked away from his house and his family. His step gradually quickening, Gabriel Calderón walked away from his God.

"What about her husband? Who was he?"

"Well, honey, that is the big family secret. No one will talk about that either."

"What do you mean?"

"I don't know if I should even talk about this, but I guess you're old enough to know the truth. She wasn't actually married to him. He was always referred to as her husband by the family, but they never married."

"Really? Aunt Pilar? Our Aunt Pilar?"

I had moved to a chair closer to my mother, my curiosity overwhelming me. It was the summer of 1977.

"Momma, she lived with him? For how long? Where? Did Grandma approve?"

"Calm down. This is not something the family talks about. You can't go asking questions of your Aunt Juanita, or your Uncle Victorio. Certainly, you must never speak of this to your Aunt Pilar."

"I promise, I promise. Tell me. I want to hear all of it."

"Well, I guess she went to live with him when she was seventeen."

"Seventeen!"

"He was forty-nine."

"Aunt Pilar?"

"Yes."

"Why didn't she just marry him. Was it because of his age?"

"*No, not his age. He was already married.*"

"*Oh, Mom! Grandma must have gone into a spin, right?*"

"*No. As I understand it, Mamá approved.*"

I leaned against the back of the chair. My family had always been so proper, so polite. Aunt Pilar was the most conservative of them. She was so quiet she could sit in a room with the family and we hardly heard her utter a word. My aunt rose even more in my estimation. Quiet, pretty, perfectly groomed Aunt Pilar. I went home to Peter that night filled with visions of romance and doomed love. My Aunt Pilar! I couldn't believe it.

CHAPTER 16

1929—Hermosillo

Pilar was ecstatic about her pregnancy. When she first told Gabriel, he seemed concerned. She disregarded it, attributing his worried look to her imagination. Of course he was happy about their child! She chose the room next to Gabriel's study and began preparing it for the baby's arrival. She would constantly interrupt his reading, pulling him into the room to show him a new addition. She did not tell her mother for several weeks, wanting to keep the news as something special she shared with Gabriel. When she did finally decide to tell the rest of the family, it was already a proven fact. She was gaining weight.

Juana came back to live with them at Rosario's insistence. Gabriel did not object. He felt Pilar was doing too much; when he had offered to bring in other help, she refused.

She had stopped attending Mass, proclaiming that she would not go to the church without him. She was aware of the gossip in town, of the resentment of Gabriel's family, his wife's bitterness, but she did not want any of this to enter into their home, and so she protected Gabriel as best she could. Gabriel, in turn, protected her. It was a conspiracy that enabled them to close out the rest of the world, and now with the

baby coming, Pilar felt they could withstand any un-
pleasantness.

The months passed and as Pilar entered into the
final weeks of her pregnancy, a lethargy overtook
her. She spent afternoons on the chaise in the courtyard. Many evenings Gabriel would sit with her in silence, holding her hand and listening to her talk on
and on about her plans for the baby.

"Gabriel, I have a name for the baby. Do you want
to hear it?"

"Of course, my darling. Anything you want to call
the baby is fine with me."

"Veronique. We will call her Veronique."

"Pilar, what if it is a boy?"

"No. It is not a boy. It is a girl, Gabriel. Her name
is Veronique."

Gabriel watched her, a smile on his face. In spite of
knowing how difficult life would be for this child in
a small village such as Hermosillo, he could not help
but take joy in Pilar's happiness. She glowed with an
obscene health. She had prepared the baby's room to
perfection, everything in pinks and yellows. She had
even made the baby's clothes, refusing to let him order a layette from Mexico City.

Late at night they would lie awake talking about
their child. She could not sleep from excitement. Instead she would sleep well into the morning, rising to
have lunch with him, then resting in the courtyard
during the afternoons.

One night he was awakened by the sound of her
crying softly. She was sitting in the corner of the
room in the rocking chair.

"Pilar, what is wrong? Are you in pain?"

He left the bed and knelt in front of her.

"Tell me."

"Oh Gabriel, I will never have this baby. I will be pregnant forever!"

"No, no. That is not true. Soon, this baby will come, I promise you that. We won't be able to stop it."

"I don't think so," she wailed. "I can't remember what it was like when I wasn't pregnant. I can't dance anymore, Gabriel. I can't even move!"

Laughing at her, he pulled her up from the chair and led her back to bed.

"Go to sleep, Pilar. The baby will come, you will dance again. We will go on a trip. I will take you anywhere you want to go. You will dance. Believe me."

"Don't you ever think of going back, Momma? To check the records? Would there be any records?"

"I don't know. I asked my brother, Victorio, about it once. He said there were records, but the church in Mexicali burned after we moved to California."

"Wouldn't there be other records? Don't you think in 1929 there would be a registry somewhere in town?"

"I never thought of that. Maybe there would be."

"Momma, why don't we go there and see? Just you and me. We could fly, or take a train. We should do it."

"No, honey. I'm certain there are no records. Victorio would have told me. He's always taken care of the family's business. He would know about any records, and he would have told me. I've certainly asked him enough times."

★ ★ ★

The sounds of Pilar's screams tore through the house and met Victorio in the entry hall. He ran upstairs. As he approached Pilar's bedroom door, Juana came out carrying linens wet with blood.

"Come with me, 'Torio. We must get more linens for the doctor. They are in the kitchen. What are you doing here? Where is Rosario?"

"She is on the way. How is Pilar?"

"It does not look good. The doctor is not hopeful for either of them. Not her, not the baby."

"Why? What is happening?"

They were in the kitchen now and she looked at him as she handed him a sack of folded linens. Her eyes had dark circles underneath. She had been at Pilar's side since her labor began yesterday. They all believed it would be a simple delivery, no doctor necessary, just Juana and the midwife, but early this morning the baby turned.

Pilar was unconscious between the pains and she had lost a lot of blood. Gabriel had not left her side, even though the doctor had tried several times to make him leave the room.

"You must help us get Gabriel out of the room, 'Torio. You must carry him out if necessary. It is going to get worse in there, and he must not witness it."

They returned to Pilar's room. Victorio himself wasn't prepared for what he saw when he entered the bedroom behind Juana. Pilar was unconscious again and ashen. Her nightgown, blood-streaked and torn, clung to her body. The doctor was waiting for the next contraction so that he could again attempt to turn the baby. Gabriel was kneeling beside the bed,

quietly sobbing and mouthing soundless words to Pilar. She did not hear, but suddenly her body arched,
her eyes snapped open, and she began to scream. The
sound careened around the room, brutally invading
every corner. The doctor tensed and made an attempt
to turn the baby. Regaining his composure, Victorio
walked behind Gabriel and bent down to him.

"Gabriel," he whispered, "you must come with
me. Now! You cannot stay in here. Pilar needs you to
go and let her do this alone. You do not belong here."

"I cannot leave her. She is dying. Can't you see
that? I will not let her die without me."

"Gabriel, I will carry you out of here if you do not
come with me now!"

Gabriel turned and looked at Victorio. Pilar's
scream had died down. She was still. Her hair was wet
with perspiration, her breathing labored.

"Please. Don't make me carry you out of here."

Gabriel stood, not letting go of Pilar's hand. He
looked around the room, then at the doctor. Gently,
he laid Pilar's hand on the sheet. Sobbing, he turned
and walked out of the room.

"What else did the family tell you about your father?"

"No one would tell me very much. Just that he and Mamá weren't married very long, and none of the family liked him. I think they wanted him to leave."

I watched my mother as she searched her memory for fragments of her father. She was quiet for a few moments, pensive. I went to the stove, refilled the teapot, then placed it back on the table.

"I remember one thing. I've always wondered about it. I was four. It was the year before Mamá and the family moved to California. I was sitting on the porch in front of the restaurant. A man walked up to me. He was carrying an ice cream cone. I remember it was hot, and the ice cream was beginning to melt. It was running down, over his fingers. He handed it to me—my first ice cream cone."

I remained silent, waiting for her to continue. Lost in her memories, she absently added another spoon of sugar to her tea and began stirring.

"For the longest time, I believed he was my father. I wanted him to be. I dreamed about him for years. Sometimes, I still do."

CHAPTER 17

When Gabriel told Pilar about the baby she did not react, she only looked at him. He tried to maintain eye contact with her, but the destruction he saw forced him to look away. He searched about the room desperately as Pilar continued to stare at him. He rose and began pacing the floor.

"When you are well, we will travel. We will take Juana, too."

Pilar followed him with her eyes. He stopped at the window and looked down into the courtyard.

"We will travel, Pilar. Go to the coast. Have you seen the ocean?"

She did not answer. Reluctantly, he turned to her. Her expression had not changed, but her eyes had filled with tears. They did not flow, but continued to build up like a river dammed. Desperate, he continued his aimless litany.

"We could go to Europe. I know you have not been there. Italy! Oh, Pilar, you would love Italy! St. Peter's Basilica, the Sistine. I want you to see the Sistine."

As he talked, he began to walk toward her.

"We could go to France. The southern coast. Pilar, it is so beautiful. You could rest there. Get well."

He approached the bed as her tears began flowing. Sitting on the edge of the bed, he reached for her.

"Everything is going to get better. I promise you, Pilar."

His mouth was buried in her hair as he said the words over and over again. Pilar, clinging to him, heard nothing.

She never cried after that first day, and, slowly, she recovered. Juana fussed over her as if she were the newborn infant. Gradually, Pilar responded. Her strength returned, but she was silent. It was the silence that brought Gabriel to the edge of despair. He watched Pilar go about the house, ghostlike and elusive. When he spoke to her, she answered him kindly, but she volunteered little of herself.

One day, he found her in the baby's room. She was sitting on the floor putting the handmade clothes into a large trunk. Patting and folding each item, one after the other, she neatly packed them. Absorbed in her task, she did not see him. Gabriel could hear her singing softly.

> *Ma chandelle est morte*
> *Je n'ai plus de feu*
> *Ouvre-moi ta porte*
> *Pour l'amour de Dieu.*

He retreated and closed the door.

In his library he opened the windows in hope of a cooling breeze, but he found no relief. Juana had placed a pitcher of lemonade on the small table, but Gabriel only stared at it dumbly. He sat in his chair and lost track of time. Gradually, the room darkened, and still he could hear Pilar humming in the next room. Juana called up the stairs that dinner was ready. He waited until he heard Pilar descend, then followed her.

PART 5

I didn't press my mother, but neither was I satisfied with my Uncle Victorio's answers. I was visiting my mother in Santa Barbara during the summer of 1977 and needed to get ready for the drive back to San Francisco. The idea to go to Mexico by myself slowly evolved as I drove into the City that evening.

I arrived at Peter's as the moon was rising. Peter wasn't home, but he had left a message for me to meet him in town for dinner. We met and enjoyed one of our long leisurely meals with lots of wine. As we were ready to leave, we noticed there was no one in the restaurant; the tables had been cleared and the waiters had gone home. The maitre d' graciously saw us out.

The fog had crept up Telegraph Hill and enclosed us in a dense, white cloud. Peter was very quiet as we got into the car. The clock on the dashboard showed 3:00 a.m. I sat in my corner of the front seat, wrapped in his overcoat, leaning against the door, watching Peter as he carefully steered the car down the hill.

We drove to Fort Point and listened to the seagulls and talked until I fell asleep in his arms. When the sun began to rise, the heat and light entering the car woke me. Peter was watching the waves, a pensive look on his face.

"Peter, have you been awake all night?"

"Yeah, I've been thinking."

"About what?"

"Lots of things, honey."

I rummaged in my purse for my comb. Sitting against the window, combing my hair, I questioned him.

"Tell me one thing you're thinking of, Peter."

He waited, watching a seagull soaring along the surface of the waves. It dipped, nearly submerging its entire body, then it rose out of the water in one smooth motion, a small fish in its mouth. It changed directions, curving and slicing through the sunrise, then disappeared behind the wall of the fort.

"I've been thinking about you, sweetheart. About us. I want you to marry me when we get back from Central America."

I put my comb back into my purse and moved along the seat until I was leaning against the steering wheel, my arms around his neck.

Teasing him, I said, "Why should I marry you?"

"Don't give me a bad time about this, Amparo. I'm serious! We won't joke about this. I want you to marry me."

I took my time. Glancing out the window, I saw the seagull make another swoop at the water. Peter, tired from being awake all night, was leaning his head back against the headrest. His eyes were closed.

"I'm waiting for your answer, Amparo."

I began undoing his tie, then unbuttoning the top button of his shirt.

"Is that better?"

"Amparo."

I whispered it. "Yes."

"Do you mean it?"

"No. I mean, yes. I mean it. I'll marry you!"

In his excitement, he began talking about his plans for a house in Marin.

"A Victorian. Three stories. With a 360-degree view of

the meadows and the ocean. Every day, we'll do whatever we want. One day, I'll choose, the next, you choose."

He held my hand as we drove home.

That night, facing him across a table at a local restaurant, I told him what I wanted to do.

"No, honey. That doesn't sound like a good idea."

"Why?"

"Why do you want to check these records?"

"To see if they exist."

"Of course they exist."

"I'm not certain of that, Peter. Why won't the family talk about it to my mother? Doesn't that sound strange to you?"

"I guess. But, it's not up to you to meddle into this."

"I don't agree."

"Well, I know that! You don't agree with anything I say."

"Peter, this is very important to me."

"Oh, hell! Do you have to put it that way?"

"I'm going to Mexico!"

The wine steward replaced the empty bottle with a new one and walked away.

"All right. Let's go to Mexico."

"Thank you, Peter! I'm so excited about this. I just know there's more to it than what they're telling Mamá."

"Well, we'll find out, won't we?"

We returned to Central America the following month. Peter was uneasy about me being with him this time, something to do with unrest in the country, people carrying guns, revolution. . . .

I could not put to rest my curiosity about my mother's origins. They were my origins. I had to know who my grandfather was, so Peter and I made plans to visit Mexico on our way back to San Francisco.

CHAPTER 1

1933—Hermosillo

Gabriel and Pilar's life together established its own cadence, revolving around their visits to see her family in Mexicali and their frequent travels to Europe. Pilar's baby sister, Teresita, was a sulky, overindulged little girl, spoiled by her adult brothers and sisters. Pilar indulged her more than the rest, bringing her dolls from France, toys from Switzerland, a clock from the Black Forest of Germany. When she and Gabriel returned from Mexicali, Pilar would be silent for several days. The traveling only provided a short-term distraction.

One morning, Pilar and Gabriel overslept due to the absence of Juana's usual noise in the kitchen. Where was the smell of her cinnamon-spiced chocolate rising to the upper floors? Pilar left the bed and, curious, descended the stairs. The silence frightened her.

Gabriel was awakened by Pilar's screams. Terrified for her, he ran down the stairs and into Juana's bedroom. Pilar was kneeling, her arms about Juana's body.

"Talk to me, please. Juana? Talk to me," she whispered.

Nearing the bed Gabriel could see that the old woman had died peacefully in her sleep.

"Pilar, she is gone. We must call the priest."

She turned and looked up at him.

"Come with me. You must get dressed. I will call the priest. Please, Pilar?"

She turned back to Juana. Placing her hand on Juana's cheek, she said to Gabriel, "I will stay here with her until you return with Father Ruiz."

Not wanting to leave her alone in the room, he placed his hands on her shoulders and tried to pull her away.

"I am all right, Gabriel. Please. Bring the priest."

Helpless to influence her, he turned and left the room.

The family arrived the following day for the funeral. Victorio, Carlos, Gabriel, and three men from the village carried Juana's coffin to the church for Mass. The family followed behind, Pilar holding Teresita by the hand. Later they all left the cemetery and returned to Pilar's house.

After their meal, Victorio asked Pilar if he could speak to her alone. She led him into the parlor while the rest of the family remained in the courtyard.

Victorio sat across from Pilar and watched her for several seconds. She had matured into an elegant and beautiful woman, composed, serene. He was in awe of her. Her gaze was steady as she looked at him, the blue of her eyes reminding him of pale velvet, soft and comforting.

"Eduardo came to see us last month."

Pilar waited for him to continue.

"He is doing very well in California. He has bought a house in a town called Santa Barbara."

He waited for her to say something, but she sat quietly across from him, an expectant look on her face. He continued, awkwardly.

"Actually, Pilar, he has bought the house for Mamá."

Her expression changed to bewilderment.

"It is a large house. He brought a photograph of it. Mamá likes it very much. There is room for the family. Everyone will be comfortable."

He continued to stumble over his words, speaking to her of schools and jobs. Pilar's expression became closed. She continued to be silent, but her body was alert, rigid. She leaned forward in her chair.

"I have arranged to sell the restaurant in Mexicali. Actually, I have received a very good offer, enough to begin another one in this new town."

Victorio arose and began pacing back and forth in front of Pilar. He continued.

"I have tried to raise the money for the train fare, but it is quite expensive, that many tickets. Of course, the children travel half fare, but still I have not been able to get enough together."

" 'Torio, Teresita will stay with me."

He continued pacing, not hearing her.

"Eduardo says there is a very nice little restaurant not far from the house. It has a bakery . . ."

"I will give you the train fare, but I want Teresita to remain here."

". . . which would be nice for Jimena. She has turned into a very good baker. We could have a panadería, combine it with our profits from the restaurant . . ."

"I will help you, 'Torio. I will give you the money for the fares . . ."

Victorio sat in a chair close to Pilar, relief on his face like a sunrise.

". . . but Teresita will stay with me."

She may as well have hit him. Stunned, he was speechless for a moment.

"You cannot be serious!"

Pilar did not reply. Her stubborn gaze locked with his. Victorio began pulling at his collar. The room was warm but she appeared to be unbothered.

Calmly, she asked him, "How much money will you need?"

He looked at the floor, then removed his handkerchief from his back pocket and wiped his forehead.

"Mamá will never let you keep Teresita here. She will insist on taking her."

Her gaze was unwavering as she continued, "How much do you need?"

"What has become of you, Pilar? How can you be so insensitive to Teresita's needs, to Mamá's? You are speaking of taking a child away from her mother."

"Yes, I am, aren't I? How much shall I remove from the bank tomorrow morning?"

"Mamá will not agree, Pilar!"

"Victorio," she replied calmly, as she rose from her chair and stood over him, "Mamá will do as you tell her, don't you think?"

"Yes. She will."

"Good. We will go to the bank tomorrow morning, 'Torio. Just you and me."

She reached over and kissed him on the cheek.

"I think it is wonderful that you will take the family to California. New beginnings, new hopes. These are fine things, 'Torio. I will miss you. All of you."

He remained in the chair, head bowed.

"I am very tired now. Will you tell Gabriel that I have gone to bed?"

Nodding his head, he answered her.

"Yes, I will tell him. Thank you, Pilar, for your help. I knew you would not fail us."

She paused at the door and, without turning back to him, she replied, "Good night, Victorio."

CHAPTER 2

October 1977—San Francisco

"There was a merry-go-round by the train station."

"A merry-go-round?"

"Yes. It was there with a small carnival, one of those shabby affairs you now see at the supermarkets. I could hear the music from the carousel as all of us got ready to board the train."

Amparo was tossing a salad on the ceramic counter in the kitchen of Peter's house. Teresita was in town for a visit.

"I had my own small suitcase, and I was wearing my green jacket. I couldn't wait to get on that train."

Amparo placed some salad on each plate and set one down in front of her mother, who was watching the surf crash against the rocks at the base of the house. The large window in the breakfast area of the kitchen gave a panoramic view of the Pacific. Today it was so gray it was difficult to distinguish the horizon. It blended with the sky as if a continuous sea beckoned to them.

"Everyone began to board. Pilar and Gabriel had come to wave us off. They were hugging and kissing all of them, and I waited for my turn. Gabriel lifted me as Mamá boarded after the others. I expected he was going to hand me to Mamá, but nothing happened. He continued to hold me as the train began pulling away. I struggled, trying to make him put me down so I could get on the train with Mamá, but he was very strong and he held on to me."

Concerned, Amparo sat at the table across from her mother. She had never heard this part of Teresita's history.

"The train pulled away without me. I remember screaming for my mother, but she only sat at the window, crying and waving to me."

"Momma. What happened then?"

"Gabriel and Pilar carried me across the street to the carnival. I think they believed it would distract me."

Teresita moved from the table to the window seat and watched the waves cresting. She was silent for a long time.

"He placed me on the carousel, strapped me to the horse. They were both smiling. We waited for the merry-go-round to begin turning. I remember throwing my arms around the neck of the horse. By then, I was inconsolable. The horse began moving up and down. Over and over. I got sick from the crying and the motion. Pilar and Gabriel were a blur as the carousel went round and round."

Amparo waited, watching her mother.

"I hate carousels. All my life, I have hated carousels. The sound of them, the music. It's an imitation of music, really. The horses aren't real. Nothing was real. My mamá had left me behind."

January 1978—La Libertad, El Salvador

I was happy to leave Central America. During the three months we were there, Peter had become too quiet. He was gone more than usual, sometimes arriving late at night or during the early morning hours. When he was at the house with me, men would arrive and Peter would take them into his study. Behind those heavy, carved oak doors, they would talk, sometimes in whispers, but always in Spanish. I became more uncomfortable and even afraid, but when I questioned Peter, he soothed my fears. Still, he did not allow me to leave the house by myself. At the end of three months, I was ready to be in a more relaxed atmosphere.

We left during the dawn hours and drove to the wharf of La Libertad to make a final check on Peter's sloop. I remained in the car with John, watching Peter through the mists board his boat and confer with the crew.

As we drove away from the dock, I told Peter how relieved I was to be leaving.

"Everyone is carrying guns. Even your crew. Why do they need guns?"

"There's going to be a revolution, Amparo. Lots of people will die. Everyone is afraid. I didn't realize how bad it was until we arrived. This has been brewing for a long time, but now I think everything here is about to explode. I won't be

bringing you with me next year, honey. I was afraid for you this time. Do you understand?"

"Yes. I understand, but, Peter, do you have to come back next year? Shouldn't you stay in San Francisco, too?"

"I have to return until I sell the plantation. I have too much money invested in it. I can't just walk away from it."

We arrived at the airstrip where Peter kept his plane. We boarded, and as we taxied down the runway, I looked out the window at the scene around me. The ramshackle building that served as the terminal was glowing as the full sunlight struck its unfinished walls. It turned a golden pink, dazzling me as if it were veneered with diamonds. As we lifted off the runway the men below became smaller, but somehow, in my memory, the rifles across their shoulders and the pistols in their belts became larger.

I looked forward to arriving in Palm Springs. We would stay in Peter's house there, visit with his friends, Richard and Alicia, before driving to Mexicali to search for records of my grandfather. I'd had no women friends to talk to for months, and I relished the opportunity to have lunch, go shopping, and gossip with a woman. My life was going to be normal again.

CHAPTER 3

They arrived very late. The house in Palm Springs was dark and sinister until Peter began turning on the lights. It was a spacious house, built to resemble an adobe. The windows were large and bare of curtains. A six-foot wall surrounded the house, guaranteeing privacy, while the tile floors radiated a welcome coolness. Amparo searched through every room until she found the master bedroom. She took her overnight bag from the rest of the suitcases and went into the cavernous bathroom. She let the brown water flow from the tap until it was clear. After pouring the bath salts into the sunken tub, she flipped the switch for the Jacuzzi. Stripping off her jeans and sweater, she tested the water with her foot, and climbed into the tub.

Later, walking through the house in her robe, Amparo relished the feel of the cold tiles on her bare feet. Realizing she had been down this corridor already, she paused and listened. Peter's voice was coming from a direction to the right. Amparo followed the sound.

"We just got in."

She entered the library. Three walls were covered from the floor to the ceiling with books. Peter was sitting behind his desk, the phone to his ear.

"About three days. We're going down into Mexico tomorrow morning."

Amparo approached a book-lined shelf and began reading titles.

"Personal business. Amparo wants to check some family records."

Taking a book about the history of Mexico down from its shelf, she looked for a place to sit.

"Of course you and Alicia will have a chance to meet her."

She spied the liquor bar behind Peter's desk and moved toward it.

"Tomorrow night? I don't know. If we get back from Mexicali. We might stay there a night."

Surveying the bottles on the silver tray, she placed her hand on a brandy. Peter turned in his chair to watch her.

"Excuse me, Richard. Amparo, honey, not the brandy. It's a hundred years old. I only have six bottles."

She picked up a brandy snifter.

"Richard, hold on, will you? Honey, don't take the bottle of brandy out of here, you hear me?"

Deftly, she moved out of his reach and smiled sweetly at him. Carrying the book, the snifter, and the bottle of brandy, she left the room.

"Amparo! Come back here, honey. Oh shit! Richard, excuse me. She's taken off with the brandy. Christ! Do you remember how much I paid for it?"

He talked to Richard for another hour, and then left the library, following Amparo's trail of lights, switching them off in each room, until he found her in the living room. She was asleep on the couch, the large book lying across her stomach, the brandy snifter still in her hand. Peter picked up the bottle from the floor, checked the contents and carefully took the glass from Amparo's hand. He placed the book on the end table and turned off the light. Lifting her from the couch, he carried her into their bedroom. He placed her on the bed and watched her as she slept.

CHAPTER 4

They reached Mexicali at noon. The registry had records of the family's restaurant, but after spending the afternoon searching through the birth records for 1928, 1929, and 1930, Peter and Amparo found nothing. They stood outside the building for several minutes trying to decide what to do next.

"There's nothing here, Peter."

"I know. You're disappointed, aren't you?"

"Of course, I am. But, I haven't given up yet. There has to be evidence of my mother's birth somewhere."

"Where did the family live before they came to Mexicali?"

"Hermosillo. But Mamá says she only lived there after they moved to California. She lived with her sister, Pilar."

"You mean your Aunt Pilar? The one who is so ill right now?"

"Yes, that one."

"Are you hungry? We didn't have lunch."

"Yes. Thirsty, too."

"Let's find a place to eat. You'll feel better on a full stomach."

They walked until they came to a restaurant. They entered and were seated beneath a large revolving ceiling fan. The coolness was a relief.

They ate in silence. Amparo finished before Peter. She looked around the restaurant, and then turned to him.

"Let's go to Hermosillo, Peter."

"Why? Your mother wasn't born there."

"Yes, I know, but my grandmother lived there before moving to Mexicali. Maybe I can find out something."

"Sure, let's go. I just don't want you to get your hopes up. I hate to see you disappointed."

"It's so difficult to give up. I just know there's an answer to all of this. He's my grandfather, you know? I only had one grandfather and I lost him when I was five. It would mean so much to me to be able to find the other one."

"We'll sleep here tonight. In the morning, we'll drive to Hermosillo. Let's go find somewhere to stay."

The following morning they drove East to Tucson, arriving late in the day. After finding a room at a hotel, they had dinner. The next morning, they were driving south to Hermosillo before the sun was rising. The Arizona desert emerged from its shadows, the mesas hovering. Cactus plants appeared to spring from the sand as the sunlight touched them one by one. Amparo watched the countryside, lost in her thoughts. They arrived in Hermosillo by midday.

"We should begin with the church. Where is it?"

"I see several. Why don't we start with the closest one?"

Amparo waited impatiently while Peter found a place to park. They entered the coolness of the church and stood waiting for their eyes to get used to the darkness. Amparo crossed herself and began walking up the aisle. A priest approached her, a greeting on his face. He was young.

"Can I help you, Señorita?"

"Father. Good afternoon. We are hoping to look at baptismal records, even birth records, if you have them."

"Is there a particular record you are looking for?"

"Yes, Father. The records of my grandfather, and of my mother."

"Yes. Please come this way. I will show you where we keep them."

Taking them into a room at the back of the church, he left them alone with several large ledgers. Amparo and Peter began the laborious task of searching for her grandfather.

It was the same in the first three churches to which they went. Hours of turning crumbling pages, reading as best they could the endless columns of names, turned up nothing. Discouraged, they left the church and walked down the street to the car. It was dark and Amparo was feeling very fatigued. Sitting in the car, she leaned her head on Peter's shoulder.

"Tomorrow, Peter, we're going to find the registry office."

"Okay."

"We'll see if we can find evidence of the title to the restaurant. Maybe something will come out of that. I'm not giving up yet."

"We'll check into everything we can think of. Okay, sweetheart?"

He waited for her answer, but she was silent.

"Amparo?"

She had fallen asleep. Peter found a hotel, and checked them in. Too tired for dinner, they went directly to their room. Long after Amparo had fallen asleep, Peter was still sitting in the chair by the window, looking out into the night.

"Look. Here it is."

"Where?"

Excitedly, Amparo pointed to the line.

"Victorio and Rosario Pérez. See, they purchased the restaurant in 1917."

"Look, there is a lien holder on the restaurant. Calderón. Gabriel Calderón."

"He was the man my Aunt Pilar lived with."

"He must have loaned them the money."

"Do you think so?"

"Sure, that's why his name is on the lien."

"That's strange."

"Why?"

"Because, Aunt Pilar would have only been about six or seven years old. She was in a convent then."

"So, she didn't live with him until later, after she came out of the convent?"

"I guess. He must have known the family before that."

"Where did they live?"

"The family?"

"No, your aunt and this Calderón."

"I don't know. Mamá says that the house was my Aunt Pilar's. I think he bought it for her."

"Did she sell it? Is it still here in town, do you think?"

"Peter, that was over fifty years ago. I doubt if she still owns it. She must have sold it by now."

Peter began turning back the pages to the beginning of the ledger. He stopped and with his finger followed each name on the page. Amparo watched him as he continued turning pages and carefully inspecting each line.

"Here it is. He purchased a house in 1928. Look, it was placed into her name two weeks later. Give me a piece of paper, honey. I want to write down the address."

"But, Peter, someone else must live in it now. We can't just go over there."

"There's no evidence that she ever sold it. It would be indicated if it was sold. The last transaction on that house took place in 1928."

CHAPTER 5

The house, entirely out of place, was standing behind a modern building. The paint had faded long ago; no one had taken care of it. They approached the front door, but as they expected, it was locked. They went around to the front of the other building. A man was sitting at a desk in an outer office.

"Excuse me, Señor. Do you know anything about the house in back?"

He lifted his head from the paper in front of him and surveyed Amparo. Then he looked at Peter.

"I do not know much, Señor."

"Who owns it?"

"A lady used to own it many years ago. No one lives in it now."

"How many years ago?"

"Before I was born, Señor. My mother spoke of the lady to me."

"Is your mother still alive?"

"No, Señor," he answered, and crossed himself.

"Does anyone take care of the house?"

"Yes."

"Do you know who it is?"

"Yes."

Peter waited for the information, but it was not forthcoming. The man returned to his paper. Peter reached into his pocket and took a twenty-dollar bill from his wallet. He offered it to the man, who rose from the chair and left the room.

"I will be right back, Señor."

He returned with an elderly man who didn't walk, but shuffled.

"Señor, can you tell us the name of the owner of the house in back?"

The old man looked at Peter and Amparo. In a barely audible voice, he answered, "Pérez. Her name is Pérez."

Amparo stepped forward and said, "That is my aunt, I think. Her name is Pilar Pérez?"

He looked her up and down slowly, and replied, "Yes, Señorita, you look like her. You have the blue eyes. I have never forgotten the blue eyes. Like the sky at midday. I saw her the first time when I came to the house with my patrón."

"Your patrón?"

"Si, Señorita. Gabriel Calderón. My patrón."

Tears were forming in the old man's eyes. He looked at Amparo helplessly.

"How old are you, Señor? What is your name?"

"I am ninety-four, Señorita. My name is Julio. I am the caretaker for the patrón's mistress. I wait for her to return."

"Do you have a key, Julio? To the house? Can we go in?"

He hesitated, concern on his withered face.

"We will not disturb anything, Julio. I just want to see my Aunt Pilar's house."

"She is still alive, Señorita?"

"Julio, my name is Amparo. Yes, she is still alive, but she is very ill now. She is dying."

He looked at her, then at Peter. He led them slowly to the house, unlocked the door, and waited outside.

CHAPTER 6

1937

Pilar was happy at last. She and Gabriel could not believe their good fortune at having Teresita with them. Hermosillo had grown larger, new schools were built, a new church, a convent. Teresita, now eight, attended the convent school, but did not live there. Gabriel would drive her to her classes every morning, and he and Pilar would return for her at the end of the day. They indulged her more than the rest of the family had.

When she became ill with chicken pox, it was Gabriel who sat up with her at night, while Pilar attended her during the day. Her room was filled with dolls, many of them imported from Europe. A lonely child, she made few friends at the convent and the other girls did not attempt to befriend her. Teresita wondered about this the first year, but gradually becoming used to her solitude, she ceased asking herself why.

She was happy, and as she grew older she was allowed to walk to the school by herself. On her way home, she often stopped at the large store owned by Gabriel. His son, Eugenio, was very unfriendly, but the store sold the best candy, so she tolerated the man's hostility.

One day, he was not in the store. In fact, the store was closed. There was a black wreath hanging on the door. Had Eugenio died? She continued home.

She entered the house and stood in the entry below the stairs. Why was it so quiet? Where was Pilar? She slowly ascended the stairs. Where was everybody? She walked down the hallway and rounded the corner of the balcony to her room. Placing her books on the desk, she picked up her Marie Antoinette doll. Hugging it to her chest, she went out to the balcony toward her sister's room.

She stood at the door and listened. There was no sound. Carefully, she turned the knob, and the door swung open. Pilar was sitting in the rocking chair in the corner of the room. Teresita entered and stood in front of her. Pilar was staring across the room, but she didn't appear to be focusing on anything.

"Pilar, what's wrong?"

She did not answer.

"Where is Gabriel? Pilar? What is happening? You look very strange."

"Gabriel is gone, Teresita."

"What did you say? I cannot hear you. You must speak louder."

Barely above a whisper, Pilar answered her.

"He is gone."

"Where did he go? I went by the store, but there was a wreath on the door. I think someone has died, Pilar. Was it Eugenio? Is that where Gabriel is?"

Pilar began shaking her head.

"No, it is not Eugenio."

"Christino, then. Is it Christino? Poor Gabriel. We will have to help him, Pilar, so he will feel better."

"You don't understand, Teresita."

Reaching up, she drew Teresita to her and pulled her into her lap. Her doll fell to the floor.

"It is Gabriel. He is dead, my darling."

Teresita could only stare at Pilar. She pulled herself away from her grasp and ran out of the room. When she reached the courtyard, she began having trouble breathing and sat down on the chaise longue. She tried to muffle her cries by burying her face into the pillows, but they came from somewhere deep inside her and wouldn't be contained. Finally, when the sobs slowed, she noticed that Pilar had already set the table where the three of them always shared their evening meal. Teresita looked up at the balcony at Pilar's bedroom door. Suddenly, she rushed up the stairs. She cautiously entered Pilar's room and sat, shamefaced, on the floor in front of her sister. Holding her knees, she spoke to the silent woman.

"Pilar, I am so sorry. You must feel very bad. What can I do?"

"Just having you here is a comfort to me, Teresita. He loved you so much, you know that, don't you?"

"Yes. He was like a father to me, Pilar. I will miss him so much."

"He was at the store when he had a heart attack. He died instantly."

"How did you find out? When did it happen?"

"This morning. Julio came to tell me this afternoon. He was here before you arrived."

Teresita put her arms around Pilar. They clung to

each other long after the room had darkened. Neither of them thought to turn on the lights. Teresita fell asleep, so Pilar lifted her and placed her on the bed, covering her with a quilt.

Leaving the room, she walked slowly down the balcony stairs to the patio. She automatically cleared the table, as if the three of them had just finished eating. In the kitchen, she filled the sink with water and carefully placed the dishes within, leaving her hands and arms in the water. Gradually, the coolness radiated to her elbows. She stood at the sink for a few more moments, then, drying her hands on a towel, she entered the dining room. Moonlight filtered through the colored glass of the peacock, freezing the image in Pilar's memory. As she neared the window, she reached out her hands like a supplicant and placed them on the iridescent breast of the bird. Leaning her face against the glass, she stood there and lost track of time. Gradually, her back and legs aching, she left the dining room and stood at the entrance to the parlor. Gabriel's newspaper and journals were lying on the floor where he had left them that morning. She began to enter the room to pick them up, but froze after the first step. Her hands shaking, she turned and left the room. Gripping the stair railing she waited for her hand to cease its tremor, then slowly climbed the stairs.

The last room she entered was Gabriel's library. His book was still open on the table next to his chair. She placed her hands on the pages, patted them, and continued circling the room. She stirred the ashes in the fireplace and replaced the poker in its stand.

On a bookshelf she found Gabriel's black quartz rosary. The crucifix was worn to a smooth silver finish. She stared at it, and with it in her hand, she walked to his chair. It was large and roomy, and when she sat in it, she was engulfed by black leather.

Hugging her shoulders, she began rocking back and forth. All night she waited for tears, but she was denied the relief.

In the morning, Teresita found her sister curled up on Gabriel's chair, his rosary on the floor. She tiptoed over to Pilar, not wanting to wake her. She picked up the rosary and placed it on a table.

The room was cold. Teresita shivered. The afghan Pilar had knitted for Gabriel last year was folded and hanging neatly on its wooden stand. She lifted it and carefully wrapped it around her sister. Pilar stirred but did not awaken.

Teresita went downstairs to the parlor. Sitting on the blue velveteen sofa, she waited while her sister slept.

CHAPTER 7

Peter and Amparo stood on a tile floor but could not discern its color. The dust was too thick. The railing leading to the upper floor was broken in several places. They stood in front of the stairs and listened to the house.

"There is a kitchen back there, and behind the staircase, a dining room. My mother told me about it."

Taking him by the hand, she led him to the back of the house. At the door behind the stairs, her hand on the knob, Amparo turned to Peter, a joyful smile on her face.

"This is the dining room. Momma says it was Aunt Pilar's favorite room."

She opened the door. Light poured through the stained-glass window as the colors reflected onto their faces. They entered and looked in awe at the peacock.

In a hushed voice, Amparo spoke.

"I was right. Oh, Peter, isn't this beautiful?"

"I've never seen anything quite like it."

He walked to the window and slowly traced the image of the magnificent bird with his eyes. Amparo followed and reached out her hand to the glass. Prisms of light burst upon her fingers. Enchanted, she placed her hand on the multicolored face of the pea-cock. The warmth drew her closer. Peter watched as she placed her face against the teal and turquoise chest of the bird. Light glistened on her hair like a kaleidoscope, breaking the strands into rainbow colors, brilliant and electric.

"Isn't this a wonderful room? Can you feel the magic?"

"Magic? I don't know about magic. Holy. Try holy. Something about this room makes you want to pray."

"Maybe they're the same thing, Peter."

At length they left the room and continued farther back into the house. Passing through the kitchen, they entered a small bedroom.

"Juana's room. This must be her room. Aunt Pilar told me about her when I was a little girl. She came over the mountains with them. She was with my Grandmother Rosario from the day she was born. I think she died in this room."

Amparo went to the closet.

"Look, Peter, there are still some clothes hanging here. Do you think they could be hers?"

"Probably. I imagine your aunt left the room as it was when she died. People did that in those days."

They continued through the house until they reached the French doors leading to the courtyard. The doorknob was rusted and came off in Amparo's hand as she turned it. Peter tried to push the doors open. They resisted. Looking down, he saw Amparo clearing years of leaves caught under them. Finally the doors creaked open and he held one of them for Amparo as they proceeded into the courtyard.

They stood in the middle of the flagstones, surrounded by a jungle of liana vines. The vines covered the pillars supporting the balcony and trailed along the stones in several layers so that as Amparo walked through them toward the stairs, they pulled at her ankles. She took off her shoes and carefully made her way to the bottom step. Peter followed her.

The shutters to Pilar's room were broken and rotted. Continuing around the balcony, carefully stepping around the liana vines, they came to the room across from her aunt's large bedroom. It was Gabriel's library.

Peter reached for a book and took it off the shelf. As he opened it, the pages crumbled in his fingers. Their edges were browned, the centers yellowed. As best he could, he replaced the book. The chair was rotted, the leather rusty and crumbled. The stuffing had become a haven for mice.

They continued into the next room.

"My mother's room, Peter. She has described it to me so many times. She once told me about the dolls. I wonder what happened to them."

"Julio? Perhaps he has granddaughters?"

"Probably."

"The bed's gone, too."

Walking around the room Amparo noticed an old trunk standing in a corner. She knelt in front of it and tried to lift the lid, but it would not budge. Peter knelt next to her and studied the lock.

"It's a steel padlock. Look, it's almost in perfect condition. No rust."

Reaching into his pocket, he took out his keys and searched through them until he found a small pick.

"What's that?"

"It's a little helper."

"For picking locks?"

"Right. I've had it since I was a kid."

"You picked locks?"

Peter looked at her. "Didn't you?"

The lock sprung open in his hand. He raised the lid for Amparo. Inside the cedar-lined trunk, the layette looked as if it had been created yesterday. No dust, no deterioration had entered during the nearly fifty years the baby clothes had lain there. Amparo lifted one of the garments.

"Oh," she breathed. "Look at this. Isn't it beautiful? Where do you think these came from?"

"Something this nice, in those days, could only come from a convent."

"You mean nuns made them?"

"Probably."

"We can't leave them here. Will the trunk fit in the car?"

"You want to take it back to San Francisco?"

"Yes."

"If that's what you want. I'll see if Julio will agree."

CHAPTER 8

1937

They waited through the following day, but nobody came to comfort Pilar and Teresita. The second morning, Julio arrived, knocking softly on the front door. Teresita answered it. Gabriel's servant stood there with grief and devastation on his face, still, he looked kindly at Teresita.

"Is your sister at home, mi'ja?"

Teresita led him into the parlor, then ran to find Pilar. Dressed in black, she held out her hand to Julio as she entered the room. Out of respect he hesitated, then took her hand briefly.

"I have come, Señora, according to my patrón's wishes."

"His wishes? I do not understand, Julio."

"Many years ago, Señor Calderón charged me with your care, should anything ever befall him."

He looked at Pilar, pleading on his face, as tears began to course down his cheeks.

"I am here now to carry out my patrón's wishes, because of love for him, and respect for you. Please, tell me how I may be of help to you, Señora, and to the little girl."

Pilar stared at him, relief beginning to build. She sat down on the sofa.

"Please, Julio, sit down. I am so glad you have come."

He looked around the room and began shaking his head.

"No, my respects, Señora, but I cannot sit down. I will stand."

"Julio, I need you to be my friend. I have no friends, now. My family is far away and Teresita and I are alone. If we are to be friends, you must sit down."

He looked at her, bewildered. As he realized the sincerity of her words, gratitude and relief flooded him. He glanced around the room again and chose a wooden chair. He moved it so that he would be facing Pilar, and sat down.

After a long silence, she said, "Tell me, Julio, about Señor Calderón. What happened?"

"He arrived at the store very early. He said he wanted to finish with the books so he could return home before Teresita arrived from school. He began to feel ill. He complained of indigestion. I suggested he could finish the books the next day. He agreed. When he arose from the desk, he suddenly had great pain in his chest. I ran downstairs to bring Eugenio. When we returned, he was already . . . he was already . . ."

He looked at Pilar, pity for her conveyed on an invisible, but tangible cloud. It passed between them and formed an understanding that would bind them together until the day she left Hermosillo.

CHAPTER 9

Together they prepared the house for closing. They covered the furniture and the mirrors, and carefully packed away Pilar's china. The silverware they took to the bank to have stored in the vault. Pilar arranged to transfer the money Gabriel had set aside for her to a bank in California. She purchased train tickets for herself and Teresita.

On the final evening, Pilar left Teresita in Julio's care and walked alone to the cemetery. It was dusk when she arrived. She searched for Gabriel's grave. Standing at the foot of the fresh mound of dirt, she spoke to him in a whisper.

"I have no tears, Gabriel. Please forgive me, I have no tears."

Kneeling, she began to dig into the mound. She continued until she reached the ground beneath. Her fingernails were broken and her black dress was soiled, but still she dug. When she had made the hole deep enough, she sat back and surveyed her work.

Turning to the side, she picked up her purse and removed a pair of scissors. Slowly, she took down her braided hair and began to undo the thick plaits. When she was finished, she knelt beside the hole and picked up the scissors. Holding her head over the now dark cavity, she put the scissors to the nape of her neck and she began to cut her hair. The hair floated, blue-black and silky, into the small pit. Patting her hair into the hole, she began to cover it. When she was finished, she stood and surveyed the cemetery. Only then could she look at Gabriel's marker. It was a massive piece of marble that read:

Gabriel Calderón
1879–1937
Cherished Husband
Beloved Father

She studied the sky, considered trying to count the stars, saw the futility of it, and, without glancing again at Gabriel's grave, left the cemetery.

CHAPTER 10

1937

Julio drove Pilar and Teresita to the train station the next day. They arrived in time for the evening train to California. As they boarded, Julio looked up at Pilar. She stood on the top step, framed in the doorway, Teresita at her side. Pilar held out her hand to Julio. He took it into both of his, and without words, said good-bye. She disappeared into the car with Teresita. Julio stood on the platform searching the windows. Finally, he saw them, Teresita with her face pressed against the window, smiling a wide grin at him. Pilar sat primly on the seat, a little in awe of her surroundings. He walked to the window and placed his hand on it, pretending to pat Teresita on the face. She began to giggle as the train pulled away.

Julio stood on the platform in the dark, long after he could no longer see the light of the caboose. Then he turned and walked slowly to the wagon. It was late now, and he was tired from the drive, but he was determined to return to Pilar's house tonight and continue carrying out his duties to his patrón.

Teresita was excited and tired. There were many people on the train. Some had pulled down the shades of their windows, preparing to sleep in their seats. Some brought out small pillows and many had blankets. Pilar placed a pillow behind Teresita's head and began to cover her with a blanket. She watched Pilar's face as the train settled into a gentle rocking motion. She had never seen this look of determination on her sister's face. Usually, she was serene, the stable influence in her and Gabriel's lives, but now her face was ungiving.

"Where are we going, Pilar?"

Pilar looked sternly at Teresita. Slowly, the tight, pinched expression on her face softened. Pulling Teresita to her, she replied serenely, "We are going home, Teresita. We are going home."

1978

Julio watched as Peter loaded the chest into the trunk of the car. Amparo stood next to him, and with a sidelong glance, Julio studied her. It was as if the patrón's love had returned, except she had not aged—certainly Julio felt every ache and pain of his ninety-four years. How was this possible? Was she as magical an entity as he had always believed? He remembered seeing her walk through the village with Juana. Her spirit was undaunted. For everyone she had a dazzling smile. Julio often wondered if he was the only one, besides the patrón, who knew of her loneliness. Now, she was leaving again, but she was taking the chest with her. This is good, thought Julio. She should never have left it behind.

He stood in front of the door to Pilar's house as

Peter and Amparo drove away. He shuffled back to his own small house down the street to await her arrival. Confused, he tried to remember where he had put the wagon and the horses. He would need them to drive her home from the train. He went in search of his daughters. They would know about the wagon.

We took the trunk back to Peter's house in Palm Springs. I put it in one of the spare bedrooms. That evening we had dinner with Richard and Alicia. I liked her instantly, and we planned a shopping trip for the following day. Peter and Richard had business to take care of, so they were both happy Alicia and I were keeping busy. I forgot the trunk.

Three days later I arrived at the adobe house laden with packages. As I spilled the parcels onto the bed, I heard Peter calling me from the other side of the house. I found him in his study.

"Honey, I'm going to have to leave for a few days. Will you be all right here with Alicia, or do you want me to have John fly you back to the City first?"

"I'll be okay here. Where are you going?"

"Back to La Libertad."

"Why?" I wailed.

"Something has come up. Richard and I have to get down there tomorrow."

I watched him. He had walked back behind his desk. Then, kneeling on the floor, he moved the chair.

"Come here, Amparo."

I walked around behind the desk. On the floor in front of him were four tiles he had removed from beneath the desk. I knelt beside him.

"This is the safe, honey. See this here? It's the dial to open it. I'm going to teach you the combination."

"Why, Peter? What's this all about?"

"I've always wanted to teach you the combination."

"Why?"

"Because you're going to be my wife, for one thing. Also, there are papers in here that I don't want anyone to know about."

"So why are you telling me?"

Exasperated, he sat back on the floor. He glanced around the room, then stared out the window. I could tell he was trying to decide what to say to me.

"Peter, what is going on?"

"Nothing, sweetheart."

"I don't believe you!"

Sighing, he got up and poured himself a drink from the bar. He motioned me to the couch and I sat down. He sat next to me and leaned back. I could see his fatigue. He had been spending too much time with Richard. Even Alicia seemed tense today at lunch.

I waited.

"Amparo, I have business down there I have to take care of. No one else can."

"What business?"

"You have to trust me, sweetheart."

I stood up and began pacing about the room.

"Do you know what I love about you?" he asked sitting up.

"No, I don't, and I don't care either."

Chuckling, he continued.

"That. Right there. That's exactly what I love about

you. You don't care. You would just as soon spit in my eye, Amparo, as know why I love you."

Leaning his head against the back of the couch again, he looked at the ceiling.

"I want to be there, Amparo, when you stand before God. Oh, I want to be there so much."

"Peter, tell me what you're up to in El Salvador."

"You're going to stand there and spit in his eye. I know you will. And he will love you for it, too. He'll be afraid not to."

"Damn it, Peter. What are you up to?"

He looked at me. I was sitting in one of the chairs across from him. I waited for his answer.

"You will have to trust me. I draw the line there. Please, baby?"

"Whatever it is, Peter, I hate what you are doing."

"I know, but I need you to believe in it anyway. Will you try to do that for me?"

"No!"

He rose from the couch and reached out his hand to me and pulled me up from the chair. He led me to the safe and showed me how to open it.

After a while, standing on the airstrip with Alicia, I could not tell the lights of the plane from the stars. They blended, and as the blue lights slowly turned white, their movement so slow, they took on the rhythm of the stars, circling as if forever in an endless sky.

Alicia dropped me at the house after asking me if I wanted to spend the night at her house. I needed to be alone. I had no premonitions, but rather I had an emptiness deep inside me. I went to the back of the house and sat on the patio for a long time. After a while I felt like a prisoner within the adobe walls. I went through the gate, dragging one of the patio lounges onto the sand. I felt better and fell asleep.

The bitter cold of the desert woke me. Shivering, I looked about. The stars were gone and the moon was on the other side of the house. I felt disoriented, as if falling into a pit. I stumbled my way in the darkness through the patio and into the house, my teeth chattering from the cold.

Standing in the hot shower, I slowly stopped shivering. I crawled into bed and was instantly asleep. I had not thought about my Grandfather Salvador for many years, but that night I dreamed about him.

He was walking toward me, his rifle lifted. He aimed and fired at me, but he missed the snake. I turned and looked at it. His head was weaving back and forth, taking aim, mouth open, fangs dripping venom. The snake struck and missed me and I watched as he sunk his fangs into the neck of the deer my grandfather was carrying. I ran to him and he lowered the wounded deer onto the ground at my feet. He tried to pull me away from the deer, but I struggled with him and threw myself upon it. I could feel the deer's heart beating, then it stopped.

I awoke with a start, covered with perspiration. I looked at the clock. It was 11:00 a.m. Peter would have arrived in La Libertad hours ago. Why hadn't he called? I picked up the telephone and dialed Alicia's number. She sounded upbeat and reassuring.

"If I know Richard and Peter, they are probably out on that sloop, their fishing poles in the water. I learned years ago it's the first place they go after they arrive. They'll call. Why don't you come over for a swim? The water's great."

"That sounds wonderful. I'll be right over."

We swam all afternoon. We had left the pool for the last

time and were lying on the lounges trying to decide where to go for dinner when the telephone rang. Alicia let the house-keeper answer it. I stayed on the lounge while Alicia went into the house to take the call. I heard her scream and for a moment I could not move. The screaming continued.

I ran into the house to find Alicia sitting on the kitchen floor, the receiver shattered beside her. The housekeeper was standing in the kitchen door staring at Alicia. In slow motion, I went into Alicia's bedroom and picked up the receiver from the table by the bed.

"This is Amparo. Who is this calling?"

"It's John, Amparo."

"What's happened? Why is Alicia screaming? Where's Peter, John? Get him on the phone!"

"I can't, Amparo. I'm sorry."

He sounded terrible, like his voice was disjointed, broken into a million pieces.

"I can't hear you very well. I think we have a bad connection, John. Where are you calling from? Where's Peter?"

"Amparo, please. I'm trying to tell you. There's been an accident. A very bad accident."

"What do you mean? What kind of accident?"

I was pacing the floor. The telephone cord kept tangling about my feet. I stood still and untangled it.

"With the boat."

I sat on the bed.

"What happened, John? Was Peter hurt? Richard? Are they okay?"

He didn't answer right away. In the pause, I quickly calculated how long it would take John to get back to Palm Springs with the plane. Too long, I thought.

"John, what commercial airlines fly into El Salvador? I'll leave as soon as I can. What hospital are they in?"

"Amparo, listen to me. I'll come and get you. I'll be there by tomorrow morning."

"That will take too long. I'll fly down tonight."

"No. Amparo, I need to tell you. God, this is so difficult. I loved that guy so much."

He began crying. Slowly, I began to understand what John was trying to tell me. I didn't realize I was collapsing onto the floor at the foot of Alicia's bed.

"John?"

"Yes."

"He's dead, isn't he?"

"Yes. God, Amparo, I am so sorry."

"How?"

"They were on the boat. It exploded about ten miles out. I didn't see it. I was back at the airstrip. The villagers told me about the explosion. Everyone was lost. There are no bodies, not even parts of the boat have washed up. The villagers have been patroling the beach since it happened, looking for debris. There's nothing, Amparo."

I waited for him to continue, but he was silent. I had crawled onto the bed, wrapped the comforter around me, and was hugging one of Alicia's feather pillows. The empty space inside of me that had begun to open last night widened until it felt as if any wind could blow through me and leave me standing.

"Amparo?"

"I'm here, John."

"What should I do? Should I stay and wait some more?" He began to cry again.

"God, Amparo. The tide's come in and gone out already. There's nothing, nothing."

"Come home, John. There's nothing any of us can do now. Come home."

"All right. I'll be there tomorrow. I'll call you when I get in."

"Yes. Please call me. We need to talk, John. I have a lot of questions."

"I know you do. I'll see you tomorrow."

We hung up. I sat on the bed, forgetting Alicia. I was cold in my wet bathing suit. I changed into my clothes, my actions automatic, programmed. I walked into the kitchen. Alicia was sitting on the floor as if in trance. The housekeeper was on a chair at the table watching her. I went to Alicia and tried to talk to her, but she did not respond.

"Greta, does she have relatives nearby?"

"Yes. There is a brother. I called him from Richard's study, while you were talking to John. Amparo, I am so sorry. Can I do anything for you?"

"Yes. Take care of Alicia until her brother gets here. John will return in the morning. I must go to Peter's house now. I can't wait for Alicia's brother. Will you do that for me?"

"You shouldn't be alone there. When her brother arrives, I will come over to stay with you."

She rose and put her arms around me.

"Is there anyone I can call for you?"

For a moment, I started to ask her to call Peter. He always took care of everything. She held me as the realization of his death spread through me. I was shaking as I left the house.

★ ★ ★

I could not stay in Peter's house, so until John arrived, I remained in the chaise lounge outside the adobe wall. He found me there, sunburned and shivering. Leading me into the house, I heard him as if he were speaking to me from a long distance.

"Amparo, what are you doing out here? Have you been here all night?"

I was unable to answer him. He led me into Peter's study and poured some brandy into a glass tumbler. I sipped it, my teeth chattering. He led me to the couch and wrapped me in the throw. Still shivering, I asked him to tell me everything.

The rest of the night, we spoke of revolution, trips in the sloop to Nicaragua, medical supplies, guns.

"Guns? Peter was smuggling guns?"

"I think so."

"Why?"

"I don't know. Peter was a quiet man. He kept so much to himself. I don't think he ever confided in anyone, except Richard."

I searched my memories for anything that could have alerted me to what he was doing, but either he was successful in keeping this from me, or I was too oblivious in my own selfishness to read the clues. Either way, I was stunned.

"Who was he smuggling the guns to, John? Do you know?"

"No. None of this makes sense to me. The villagers said he and Richard took some other people onto the boat with them. There were two of them, strangers. No one got a close look. The boat left, heading towards Nicaragua. About ten miles out, it exploded. The explosion was too large to be caused by the engines."

Silently, I stared at John.

"Amparo, I think someone wanted him dead."

He waited for me to reply, but I was unable to speak. In my mind, doors were closing, slamming shut. Echoes of silence ricocheted through my brain. John disappeared from my sight, then the room slowly vanished.

We stayed in the house for several weeks. Lucidity visited me briefly. It would return to check on me, take note of the terrain, and shaking its head, disappear again.

I remember my mother was there. The rest of my family came and went. John was always there. My bath water would overflow, as I would forget I had begun to fill the tub. John would turn off the water and wipe up the floor. He made me eat, and later he took the massive oak doors to the study off their hinges to find me inside, unconscious on the couch, Peter's brandy gone.

I spent the long nights crying, John holding me, telling me everything would be all right. But I knew better. Nothing was ever going to be all right again. A doctor's needle finally gave me peace, and John the rest he needed.

When I finally woke, it was midafternoon. Through the window, I could see John sitting in the patio, his head in his hands. He had not shaved during the weeks since Peter's death. He was haggard, his eyes red-rimmed. I went out to the patio and knelt before him.

"You look like hell, Amparo."

Placing my cheek against his knee, I replied, "You look worse."

He sucked on a cigarette like it was a lifeline, then threw it across the yard. His hand on my head, he replied,

"Are you all right now?"

"No, I'll never be all right."

He waited silently, studying the sky, looking for help.

"He was supposed to live forever, John."

"I know. I know."

"I thought he would live forever."

"No one does, Amparo. What are you going to do now?"

"I don't know."

"The house in San Francisco is yours. Did you know that? So is the plane."

"How do you know?"

"Peter's attorney was here. He talked to your brother. He didn't want to impose on you, so he made arrangements with your brother."

"Maybe I'll give them away."

"Peter always said you would."

I was sitting on the ground in front of him. He lit another cigarette and looked at me.

"Amparo, go take a bath, honey. You really look like hell."

"You've been a good friend to me, John."

"Someone has to be a friend to you, Amparo. Actually, you need a goddamn keeper. Go take a bath. You'll feel better. I'll take you to dinner. We'll go see Alicia. She's been worried about you. I'll call your mother while you're getting ready. Go on."

CHAPTER 11

Fresh from her bath and wrapped in a clean bathrobe, hair dripping, Amparo looked throughout the house for John. Searching the east wing, she heard water running and followed the sound. She entered the spare bedroom and realized this was where John had been sleeping. The bathroom door was ajar. Amparo slowly approached it as she continued drying her hair with a towel. Pressing her fingers against the door, she called out softly.

"John? Are you in here?"

There was no answer. She pushed the door open slightly.

"John?"

She heard what sounded like sobbing. The bathroom was filled with steam. As she entered, the sobbing grew louder. He was standing behind the opaque shower door, his hands on the wall opposite the shower spray. The water was pouring on his back and he appeared to be holding himself up, leaning on the wall and crying.

Amparo watched him for a moment, then she walked across the room toward the shower. John did not hear her. She dropped her towel and took off her terry robe. Gently, she opened the shower door and entered the large tiled stall. Her back against the tile wall, she worked herself between John's arms, and up until she was facing him. Putting her arms around his neck, she began whispering in his ear, but he could not hear her. He opened his eyes and looked at her, amazed, as the water ran like a small river over their bodies. He pulled her to him and buried his face in her hair. As she began kissing him, his sobs transferred to her until they were crying together. He reached behind him and turned off the water, then he lowered her to the tile floor.

CHAPTER 12

Three days later, John awoke and reached for Amparo, but the bed was empty. He looked at the clock. It was 6:15 a.m. He rose and searched for her, finding her on the patio by the pool. She had already been swimming and was now resting on the chaise. He sat on the edge of the chaise and looked at her.

"Want some coffee?"

"Sure. You're up early."

He walked to the table and poured himself a cup, then returned to a chair near her. He sat and quietly stirred his coffee, remaining still and waiting for Amparo to speak.

"John, can I leave the plane here in Palm Springs?"

"Depends."

"On what?"

"On whether you will be using it immediately. Do you want me to fly you somewhere?"

"No."

He waited, taking sips of his coffee.

"Can it be left in San Francisco?"

"Yes. Peter leased a space for it. It's where he kept it when he wasn't using it."

"Could I sell it?"

He reached over and placed his cup on the table, then turned back to Amparo. He didn't answer her.

"Are they easy to sell?"

"What is this, Amparo?"

"I don't want to keep the plane."

"Why?"

"I don't think I will be going anywhere for a while. There is no place I want to go."

He walked over to the pool and looked into the water. It was a few moments before he realized it was the color of her eyes. He turned and walked back to her. He knelt beside the chaise and tried to take her hand, but she gently pulled it away.

"Honey, you don't have to feel bad about what has happened between us. I care about you so much. God, I love you."

"I don't feel bad."

"Then, what's wrong. Why are you acting this way?"

"I have to get back to the City. There are so many things I have to take care of. I'm just trying to decide what to do with the plane."

He was silent, looking at her hands. She was holding an empty coffee cup and turned to put it on the patio floor beside her.

"I just don't want to keep the plane, John."

"All right. We don't have to keep it. We'll sell it. That won't be a problem."

She looked at him and removed her sunglasses.

"We're not going to sell it, John. I'm going to sell it."

"That's what I meant."

"Then, I'm going to close the house in San Francisco."

"Are you going to sell it, too?"

"No. I don't think I could ever give it up. I just want to close it for a while."

"Then, what are you going to do? No plane. No pilot." He waited for her reply, barely breathing.

"Right."

"God damn it, Amparo. What are you talking about?"

He had risen from the floor and was pacing along the edge of the pool. She waited until he stood in front of her again.

"I think you know. Let's not do this, John."

"Do what? Do what, God damn it?"

"Argue about this. Please?"

"Oh! I see. At least, I think I see. Do I have it right? You're going back to the City, without the plane and I can go to hell. Is that it? Do I have it right?"

He turned his back on her and stared at the pool again. She spoke to his back.

"No. That's not right. At least, you're wrong about the hell part."

He turned back to her, a look of devastation on his face.

"No, Amparo. I'm right about the hell part. It's the only thing here I have been right about."

"I'm sorry, John."

He sat in the chair facing her again. He felt drained.

"Honey, you mustn't do this. You mustn't be alone. You need taking care of. Let me do that."

"I don't need taking care of, John."

He placed his head in his hands.

"Christ! I can't believe you're doing this. What about the last three days? What about that? Do you think this has meant nothing to me? Didn't it mean anything?"

"Of course, it did. It was wonderful, John."

"Wonderful! That's all? Wonderful?"

She looked at him helplessly.

"Amparo, I love you. I can't just walk away from you. Not now. Not after what's happened between us. Please? Don't do this!"

"I've been out here since sunrise, trying to see my way around this, but it's what I want."

"What? What do you want? Tell me. I'll get anything you want, do anything . . ."

"I want to be alone, John. I need to be alone."

He didn't reply. Sitting in the chair, he stared at her, disbelief slowly turning to anger. He rose and went into the house.

Soon, Amparo heard the front door slam. She listened to the sound of his jeep as it roared down the street.

She walked slowly through the empty house, saw that his belongings were gone, then returned to the patio. She remained there alone until after dark. It wasn't until the following morning that she remembered the trunk.

CHAPTER 13

The lid creaked as it had the first time she opened it. Still, there was no dust. Amparo began taking out the top layer of garments. They were exquisite, each hand-sewn, the lace handmade. The fabric was soft, like old silk. She sensed that the fabric felt this way when it was new. Small dresses in white were trimmed with ecru lace and embroidered with pastel-colored silk threads. They were feather light, as if angels had breathed substance into them. Carefully, she placed each piece on the carpet beside her. When she had taken half the garments out of the trunk, she came to a small box nestled in the folds of an angora baby blanket. Amparo lifted it out and opened it.

The pearls were alive, breathing. They reflected the pale gray of her slacks. Opera length, they were perfectly matched and glistened in the afternoon light.

She continued taking out the baby garments. On the bottom of the trunk, she found a piece of paper. Yellowed, the folds were cracked. Carefully, she lifted it out of the trunk and watched it fall into four pieces, as if neatly clipped along the creases. She pieced them together on the carpet. It looked like an official record, but it was written in Spanish. She tried to define the words. All she could discern were the names of Gabriel Calderón and Pilar Pérez. Looking towards the bottom of the form, she deciphered another name. *Veronique Angelique Calderón*. The birth date showed December 15, 1929. Amparo leaned against the wall next to the chest.

Aunt Pilar's baby. This was her birth certificate. These were her clothes. Slowly, she began to realize what she had found. Veronique was born the same day as her mother, Teresita. How can that be? Well, she thought, it's possible. They could have had the babies the same day. Her mother, Teresita, survived; little Veronique did not.

She looked at the paper again. There must be a space for cause of death. The baby had died at birth, everyone had said that. So, where did the paper show this?

She reached for the telephone and called Alicia.

"Hello?"

"Alicia, this is Amparo."

"How are you? Are you all right? I've been worried about you."

"I'm sorry. I'm okay. What about you?"

"Managing. Richard left everything in order. I have nothing to do, Amparo. I'm thinking of selling the house. What about you?"

"I don't know yet. Alicia, do you speak Spanish?"

"Of course. Don't you?"

"No. I have a paper I need you to read to me. Can I come over right now? Are you busy?"

"Are you kidding? Of course, come over. It will be good to see you."

Alicia's house was cool, in shadows. The curtains were drawn. Alicia's face was haggard, but she smiled at Amparo and wrapped her in a welcoming embrace.

"Let me see the paper."

Amparo took the pieces out of her purse and handed them to her.

"It's a birth certificate. Where did you find it?"

"In a trunk. Can you read it to me?"

"It says, let me see, it says *Veronique Angelique* was born to Gabriel Calderón and Pilar Pérez on December 15, 1929."

"Yes, I know that, but does it say anything about the baby dying?"

Alicia scanned the paper.

"No."

"Are you certain?"

She scanned it again.

"Nothing. This baby didn't die. At least, not according to this paper." She handed it back to Amparo.

"Who are these people, Amparo? Relatives?"

"Yes."

"The ones you were looking for two months ago, when you and Peter arrived?"

"Yes, the ones."

Amparo stood and hugged Alicia.

"I've got to go. Thanks. You've helped me a lot."

"Won't you stay for lunch? We haven't talked for a while."

"When I get back?"

"Back from where? Where are you going?"

"To talk to a man."

"What man? Amparo, wait a minute."

On the porch now, she hugged Alicia again.

"The only man who can tell me about this paper. I'll be back in a few days."

CHAPTER 14

Amparo went home and packed quickly, taking only enough clothing for a few days' trip. She reached the coast of San Diego in the late afternoon and struggled through the commuter traffic until she was driving north on Route 1. The sun was a great glowing pumpkin as it slowly sank behind the horizon. It turned the ocean a vivid copper, the crests of the waves gilded with gold. She drove into the night and arrived at her Aunt Jimena's in Santa Barbara long after the dinner hour.

There was no place to park in front of the house. She walked the block and a half to the front yard. The lights in the kitchen were still on, but the rest of the house was in darkness.

Jimena opened the door only a few inches and peeked out.

"It's me, Aunt Jimena, Amparo."

Surprised, she opened the door wider.

"Amparo, my goodness. It is you. Come in. It is late. Are you alone?"

"Yes, it's just me. I came alone."

She looked around Amparo and out the door.

"Where is your car?"

"I parked it up the street."

"Oh."

She stood awkwardly, studying Amparo. Jimena

was very old now. She seemed smaller than Amparo remembered her.

"How is Uncle Victorio, Aunt Jimena? Is he well?"

"Yes, mi'ja. He is fine. He is very old, very old. He does not leave the house anymore. But the children come, they bring groceries. Sometimes, one of them will drive me to the store, but I get tired now, honey. Have you eaten?"

"No, but I'm not hungry."

"But, you must eat, mi'ja! You are too thin."

"Maybe in a moment I'll have something. Is Uncle Victorio awake? Can I see him? Talk to him?"

"Yes. He is awake. He's watching television in the bedroom. Come, I will take you to him."

Jimena led her through the darkened house. The living room was as Amparo had always remembered it. There was a large crucifix on the far wall. Beneath it was a small altar where two candles burned in their tiny crystal cups. The same serape was draped over the back of the green couch, and on the table in front was a pair of porcelain flamenco dancers. Amparo paused to touch them, then she continued through the room.

His back to the door, her uncle was sitting in a large easy chair. A blanket was wrapped about his legs. He seemed to be asleep in front of the television, but when Jimena turned it off, he started.

" 'Torio, look. Amparo has come to see us. Isn't it wonderful? It is Amparo."

He turned and looked up at her. At seventy-two he was alert and smiling. His hands were bent and gnarled from arthritis, but he lifted one to her in the formal handshake he had used all his life to greet Amparo and her brothers.

"Uncle Victorio? Good evening. How are you, sir?"

Jimena brought a chair from the other side of the room and placed it behind her. Victorio waved her into it. As she sat down, he studied her. He looked at Jimena briefly, then she left the room.

"Amparo? How are you? Your mother told me about your novio. We were so sorry to hear about what happened. Can I do anything for you? Do you need anything?"

"No, Uncle Victorio. There is nothing I need."

"Peter took care to see you will want for nothing?"

"Yes, sir. He did."

"Good. Good."

He appeared to doze off again, so she waited. Nervous, she glanced around the room. Every available space was covered with framed pictures of the family. She saw herself nestled in her Aunt Pilar's arms, her baptismal gown trailing to the floor. Her high school graduation picture was among his children's, along with her brothers'. She stood in her cap and gown between her parents and Pilar. There she was in her bridal gown at the entrance to the church, Pilar adjusting her veil, her mother behind her, straightening out the train of her dress. She turned and watched her uncle sleep. She waited. He awoke again about thirty minutes later. He looked at her, and for a moment it seemed he didn't recognize her.

"Pilar?"

"No, it's Amparo."

"Yes, of course."

"Have you been able to see her, Uncle Victorio, visit with her?"

"Two months ago, Consuelo took us. She is like a child again. Have you seen her?"

"Not for several months. I plan to see her soon."

"Good. Good."

"Uncle Victorio, it is Aunt Pilar I've come to see you about. I need to ask you a question."

He looked at her warily.

"What question?"

She reached into her purse and removed the birth certificate. Carefully, she placed the pieces in his lap, arranging them so that the light reflected upon the writing. He reached for his glasses and slowly and painfully wrapped them around his face. He read the papers and his face became closed and gray. He looked at Amparo sternly, and she was just as frightened of him then as she was when she was a child. Sitting in his chair, he was still an imposing man, dominating, controlling everyone in his line of vision.

"Where did you get this, Amparo?"

"From a chest of baby clothes."

"What chest? What clothes?"

"I found the chest in Aunt Pilar's house. In Mexico."

"Hermosillo?" he roared at her.

Aunt Jimena came rushing into the room at the sound of his outrage. He waved her away imperiously. She left the room again.

He looked at her above his reading glasses, as she

felt herself growing smaller and smaller. Bravely, she continued.

"Was Veronique Pilar's baby girl?"

He stared down at the papers, almost sulking. She thought he had fallen asleep again.

"Yes. Veronique was her baby."

"What really happened to Veronique? Where is she?"

He looked at her again, bewildered.

"I don't know where she is," he replied, like a stubborn child.

"Uncle Victorio, I think you do. I think you are the only one who can tell me about Veronique. Please?"

"You meddle where you shouldn't. These things happened a long time ago. Long before you were born. Before the family came here from Mexico."

"I know, but I need to know about Veronique. There is no mention of her death on this certificate. What happened to her? Who is she, Uncle Victorio?"

He remained silent. His head bent down onto his chest, he was trying to withstand the onslaught of her curiosity.

"Amparo, some things are better left alone. This is one of them."

"No. I cannot accept that. I think I know who she is, this Veronique. But, I need you to tell me. I need to know the truth. Please, Uncle Victorio?"

The papers in his lap took on a life of their own. They shone yellow in the lamplight, and as he shifted in his chair, discomfort prodding him, they drifted to the floor. He stared at them accusingly, then turned the gaze on Amparo. She waited, and he began telling her.

"The night she was born, I had driven all day and night from Mexicali. Mamá had come with me, but she wanted to stop at the church to pray, so I left her there and went on to Pilar's house. When I arrived, everyone was in the bedroom with Pilar. There was blood everywhere, and she was screaming. Gabriel wouldn't leave her. They were dying, we all thought they were dying . . ."

CHAPTER 15

December 15, 1929

In the study, Victorio poured Gabriel some tequila and then poured himself a glass.

"Here we are again, my friend."

Lifting his glass to Gabriel, he drank. Gabriel only stared at his glass on the table.

"We must talk. I have spoken with my mother and she agrees with my decision."

Exhausted, Gabriel looked at Victorio.

"What decision?"

"The decision I have made for the baby."

Gabriel shook his head as if to wake himself.

"What in the hell are you talking about, Victorio?"

"I cannot allow Pilar to raise this baby."

Gabriel was fully alert now. Victorio took another gulp of the tequila and continued.

"You cannot give this baby your name. The church will not baptize him."

Gabriel glared at Victorio. The first time he had met the younger man, this same look of determination was on his face. Gabriel was stunned. He could not think of anything to say.

"The baby will have the Peréz name. He will be baptized in the church in Mexicali. Pilar will be his sister."

Gabriel began to laugh softly. He continued until he realized he was near hysteria. Abruptly, he answered Victorio.

"I will not allow it. No one is taking Pilar's baby from her. It will kill her."

"You really have nothing to say about it, Gabriel. It is a family matter. I make the decisions for this family. You don't."

"Pilar will not agree."

"Pilar will do as I tell her to do, as Mamá tells her to do. We will take the baby to Mexicali as soon as he is born."

"That is preposterous. I will not allow it. You will not take her baby out of this house."

"Who will listen to you, Gabriel? Who will defend you? The church? The priest? Who will support you?"

"How can you be so cruel, Victorio? How can you do this to Pilar? Don't you realize what you are doing? What will you tell the baby? That his mother is Rosario? Who will accept that?"

"Gabriel, let me remind you. The agreement was for you to have Pilar. The agreement was for there to be no children. Why weren't we told about this baby when something could have been done? Why did we learn so late?"

"She did not tell me until she was many weeks along. It was too late. And even if it hadn't been too late, I would not have allowed her to abort this baby. She is too happy about it."

There was an eerie silence coming from Pilar's

room. Gabriel hurried across the hall in time to see Rosario emerge carrying the baby.

"It is a baby girl, Gabriel. Come, see her."

He looked at his daughter. She was very tiny. Even his sons had not been this small.

"Is Pilar all right? I must go to her."

"No. You must not go in there. Juana and the doctor are caring for her. That is what she needs right now. She is not conscious."

Gabriel turned to Victorio standing behind him.

"Have you told him, 'Torio?"

"Yes, Mamá."

"Rosario, you must not take the baby from Pilar. It will destroy her."

"Gabriel, the baby is the one I am thinking of. She must not know Pilar is her mother. She must not have that burden. You know we are right."

"Won't you wait before you take her? Let Pilar see her?"

"When Pilar is well again, you must bring her to Mexicali to see the baby, Gabriel. You must bring her often to see her baby sister, Teresita."

Turning, Rosario took the baby down the stairs and through the front door. Victorio followed her.

Gabriel hurried down the stairs after them. He stood in the open doorway and watched them drive away into the darkness. Bewildered, he walked into the room Pilar had set up as a small chapel. He knelt at her prie-dieu. His face in his hands, he began a litany.

"Her name is Veronique. Her name is Veronique. Please, God, her name is Veronique."

He remained at the prie-dieu until the early morning hours. As the sun rose, he slowly climbed the stairs to Pilar's room.

CHAPTER 16

In silence, Amparo watched her uncle. Tears streamed down his face, falling onto his faded sweater. His hands, helpless and crippled, lay in his lap. The blanket had slipped onto the floor. She reached down and lifted it. Wrapping it around his knees, she placed his hands upon it. They were cold, so she continued to hold them, trying to warm them.

"Uncle Victorio? It's okay. It will be okay."

"No. Amparo, I did a terrible thing. Lies. We have lived with lies. All of us. And Pilar. I hurt her so much."

"You thought you were doing the right thing, and you did. Uncle Victorio, please believe me."

"You will tell your mother? You will tell Teresita? You will explain? There was nothing I could do. I could not let her grow up knowing. The people in the village were so cruel. That is one of the reasons I took the family to Mexicali, to escape the gossip, the slander."

She continued to hold his hands, wrapping them in the blanket. They were beginning to warm.

"When we came to California, Pilar would not let us take Teresita. Mamá was heartbroken, and Teresita, she cried so much. But you see, Amparo, Pilar loved her little girl. She would not be separated from her.

You must tell your mother. She was not abandoned. Pilar never abandoned her."

He was pleading with her now, and she saw an old, old man in need of redemption. She put her arms around him, held him close, her face next to his.

"Uncle Victorio, listen to me," she whispered. "You have freed Pilar. You have freed Teresita. Do you understand?"

He looked up at her, and began nodding his head. Amparo kissed him and bid him good-bye.

At the door, she heard his voice, once again commanding. There were hints of the old imperiousness in the tones.

"Amparo!"

Her back to him, she was at the door. She stopped, leaned her head against it, and held her breath.

"Yes, Uncle Victorio."

"Today, Amparo, you have set us all free."

She held her face against the door for a moment, feeling the rough wood rubbing against her cheek. Exhaling in relief, she left the room.

EPILOGUE

1978 - Hermosillo

My Grandmother Pilar died two weeks ago. She died peacefully in her sleep, crept away silently while I was standing by her bed. I held her hand even after the nurse had disconnected the heart monitor. My mother smoothed Pilar's forehead, and then combed her hair, unplaiting the braid and letting the silver hair fall free. I left the room so that Mamá could be alone with her.

At her funeral, my brothers and Uncle Victorio's sons were her pallbearers. There was not an open coffin at her grave, but at the funeral home, before the coffin was sealed, I removed Pilar's crystal rosary and replaced it with Gabriel's. Now, I hold her rosary in my hands as I sit in Pilar's house. Julio allowed me back into the house only last night. The paint has dried, the stairs are repaired, the balcony rebuilt. The rosary catches the light here in the dining room and throws the reflection back at the stained-glass window—a defiance never lost, a tradition held precious as diamonds. There is so much I understand.

My Grandmother Isobel on my wedding day told me to never forget who I am, or where I come from. I understand now the things of which she spoke. Traditions make us strong. Traditions are the anchors that will save us when the world begins its final spin. Traditions of survival, of perseverance, of love are what I will pass on to the child within me.

John says his name is also important, and that I should

marry him so that my child will have a name. But I am not certain John is the father. This may be Peter's child. John says it doesn't matter. It is the only thing on which we agree. After he left, angry for the final time, I remained on Pilar's patio long after dark.

This morning, as I went upstairs, I slid my fingers along the newly polished balustrade, feeling the silkiness, letting each finger curve along the surface. Following the voices of the workmen, I went to the balcony and looked into the courtyard.

"No. Not there. The rose bush goes by that wall. Yes, there. And the orchids, over here. See? Yes, like that."

I stepped down to the patio to join Julio while he continued to direct the gardeners. He turned and watched me descend the stairs.

"Be careful, Señorita Pilar. The patrón will not want you to fall. He will hold me responsible."

He hurriedly shuffled over to me, a look of distress on his face.

"It is me, Amparo. Julio, I am Amparo, remember? I have something to tell you. Please come and sit with me."

We sat at the new table he had placed to the left of the French doors. I had not felt it was the best place for the table, in the direct line of any traffic coming through the doors, but he had insisted.

"Julio, do you remember Teresita, my mother?"

Watching the gardeners, he nodded to me, so I continued.

"Her mother, my Grandmother Pilar, passed away several days ago. I've waited to tell you, because I've been afraid the news would upset you."

He continued to nod, not taking his eyes off the gardeners.

"Pilar, Julio. It is Pilar who has passed away."

He looked at me, his eyes rheumy, tearing. He considered me for a moment, studying me closely like a blind man trying to sense a clue.

"Señorita, I have arranged for someone to come and fix the kitchen so the water will run again. He will be here before the patrón returns for his dinner. You must rest now. The child comes soon. We have much to do before your child arrives."

"Julio, look at me. I am Amparo."

"Yes, I know, Señorita. Your name means refuge. Amparo. Have I told you about the first day your grandfather saw your grandmother?"

"Yes, you have, Julio."

"Your grandmother, she was very beautiful, very young, vibrant."

The plumber had arrived. We rose and together entered the house to let him in. Julio reached up and placed his arm around my shoulder. Partly supporting him, and he supporting me, we continued through the hall.

"Señor Calderón fell in love with her. How could he help himself? Every man in the village was in love with her. She would walk into a room, and the walls would sing, like an angels' chorus. Angels' voices. . . ."

So now I sit here alone amidst the fragrances of my grandmother's garden. The jasmine is heady and rich, overpowering the delicacy of the roses. Lianas climb the adobe pillars and weave their way along the balustrade. A light breeze has entered the patio and leads the plants in a whispering chorus. I had to sneak past Julio asleep in Juana's room. Soon my child will be born, and when she arrives, the ghosts who keep me company will be dispelled. My Grandfather Gabriel can be at peace, and my Grandmother Pilar can rejoice.

This child will not be born with a shadow on her soul. I don't know who her father is, but then, it doesn't matter. I know who her mother is, and so will she.

About the Author

Sylvia López-Medina is a writer who lives in
Santa Cruz, California.